AF410217

MALARKEY'S IMAGINOMNIBUS

They Walk Among Us

An Urban Fantasy Anthology

THESULK.COM

*For everyone who wonders about the
things we don't see*

CONTENTS

WELCOME TO MALARKEY'S IMAGINOMNIBUS

Greetings reader, welcome to Malarkey's ImaginOmnibus. Allow us to escort you to your seat while you leaf through these pages, or perhaps slide through them on your electronic reading implement of choice. Within these words, you will find witches, demons, ghosts, dragons, creatures of the night, a selection to cause delight.

Be warned. There lies within; violence, death, adult content, references to mental health, suicide, and horror elements.

From thirteen authors, we bring you tales of those things that walk among us. The inexplicable, the strange, and perhaps deranged. What lies behind the every day, the mundane reality that coats our world in a veneer of easy-to-digest simplicity? We bring you thirteen tales that just might be true, to enable you to see things anew.

A note. Our authors come from far and wide, and each tale is unique, delivered with an original voice, and so we have decided that language should be of their own jurisdiction. For this reason, you may note that the English used pertains to the location of the author. Stories may be in British, Australian, Canadian, or United States, written English conventions. It may not matter to you, but it's something we felt we should mention, in case it causes consternation.

So reader, without further preamble, lest this introduction causes unneeded delay, we invite you to turn the pages, do come and play.

Mirror, Mirror

Evelyn Chartres

*T*he rain pattered against Laura's car roof, like a polite clap at a formal function. Meanwhile, a sultry brunette with her piano played on the radio. Laura loved the Siren, but hearing the line about a man who 'rubs his wedding finger without a wedding band' was hitting too close to home tonight.

"Sorry," Laura said to herself, and changed the channel. "I'm not feeling this."

She returned her hands to the four and eight positions and focused on the downpour ahead. The rain glistened in her headlights, reminding her of a myriad of falling diamonds. While pretty, the glare from the oncoming traffic caused the white lines to fade and challenged her to stay in her lane.

Laura hated driving at night, a time when travelling along a deserted highway was deceptively serene. Just beyond the silver light of her headlights there could be a herd of deer waiting to make an appearance. It was not so bad in the city, but thinking about it made her blood pressure rise.

"Stop it," Laura scolded herself.

After taking a series of controlled breaths, the tension around her forehead eased. The last thing she needed after this day was being forced to turn back on account of a stress-induced migraine. *Left to suffer in silence in a home filled with lies.*

"Time to get out of this city," Laura added to further focus her thoughts.

She needed to seek refuge at her family cabin. However, Laura wondered if this day was done with her. This went beyond waking up on the wrong side of the bed, stubbing her toe on her way to the shower, or putting a run in her favourite stockings. Although, by adding burning her tongue on the scalding-hot coffee to the equation, it described the first hour of her day perfectly.

The rain transitioned to a thundering applause that drowned out the music from the radio entirely. Laura fiddled with her controls to increase the speed of her wipers but flipped them to '*Intermittent.*' Soon there was a thick sheet of water running over the entirety of her car.

"Crap," Laura said.

She flicked the lever twice. The wipers blurred as they travelled back and forth across the glass. That was when she realised those distorted lights were actually red and blue lights from a police cruiser blocking the road.

"Fuck!" Laura swore.

She slammed on the brakes, and the sound of jackhammers assaulted her ears. As the cruiser grew bigger in her field of view, the car's rear end vied for a first-place finish in this unexpected race.

Laura turned the wheels to compensate. Fearing the worst, she buried her nails into the steering wheel and tensed up, but stopped at a ninety-degree angle to the cruiser. While gasping for air, there came a tapping at her window.

She lowered the window. Rain immediately poured into the cabin and soaked her left side. *That's just peachy.*

An officer wearing a yellow rain jacket and a black peaked cap stood there with hunched shoulders. He shone a large flashlight at her face before searching the cabin. The rain that dripped off his cap, nose, and lower lip made her empathise—or it did, until the icy rainwater seeped into her nether region. *That's not what I needed…*

"The road is closed," the officer said. "Did you have anything to drink tonight?"

"Nothing since lunch," Laura said honestly.

The officer's neutral features were replaced by a cocked brow and tilted head. Water pooled on the brim of his cap, drizzled down his face and neck.

She picked up on his confusion, blushed, and added, "I accidentally switched off my wipers. I didn't realise you were there until it was nearly too late."

"Are you good to drive?" the officer asked.

"I'm fine," Laura replied. "Why is the road closed?"

"The water's a metre deep up ahead," the officer replied.

"Oh—" Laura said.

"You need to get off at this exit," the officer said while pointing to his left. "You'll follow the signs to get back on the highway."

Laura looked at her rearview mirror and spotted the exit number. It led to a part of the city she seldom heard of and never visited.

"Ma'am?" the officer asked as Laura turned two shades paler.

"I'm fine," Laura lied. "So, just follow the signs?"

"That's it," the officer said with a smile.

"Thank you," Laura said and smiled before closing her window.

Laura lowered her head and let out a deep breath. She had no reason to be anxious, and yet her heart was at a gallop. It took her several controlled breaths for her hands to steady. She grabbed the wheel, pushed down on the throttle, and steered toward the exit.

"It's not like I have a choice," Laura said.

* * *

"Just follow the signs," Laura mimicked sarcastically.

The exit led down to a commercial development filled with warehouses and nameless storefronts. It was easy enough to get lost in broad daylight when faced with endless nondescript street names and buildings. Under the cover of night, it was nearly guaranteed.

There were no signs at the bottom of the ramp, so she turned right instead of heading under the overpass. After six streetlights and three four-way stops, Laura had yet to come across a single sign.

"I should've taken a left and got on the ramp and headed back home," Laura said.

Thirty minutes ago, the idea of going back home would have taken the wind out of her sails. After roaming around this urban maze, the notion lifted her spirits noticeably. Just the idea of getting out of her damp clothes and hiding under her covers led a smile to creep across those lips.

"To hell with playing hide-and-seek with these signs!" Laura snapped.

She hugged the right side before turning hard to her left for a U-turn. Laura misjudged the street width and jumped the curb before the wheel settled on the asphalt. She rocked back and forth in the driver's seat and her seatbelt locked, but she was no worse for wear.

After a light turned green, she caught a periodic thump. As she eased off the accelerator, the frequency changed. The sound transitioned to flapping, and she had to fight her car from veering right.

"No—No—No—No—No!" Laura yelled.

She brought the car to a stop and turned on her hazard lights. She was alone at night, in an unfamiliar area of the city, and had a flat tyre to boot. *Which deity did I piss off?*

"This sounds like the premise for a horror movie," Laura said after taking a decidedly dim view of the situation.

She looked out through her windshield as a curtain of rain approached and enveloped her. The car shook violently before tapering off just in time for another wave to overtake her. Given the weather, Laura knew she would be hard pressed to get the bolts off the wheel.

"I need help," Laura said.

Laura reached into her glove compartment. She rummaged around for what appeared to be an eternity. After clearing out most of the contents that left a mess piled up on the passenger-side seat, she found a card with a phone number.

"I'm glad the car's still under warranty," Laura said before dialling the number for roadside assistance.

* * *

"What do you mean, you *might* send someone out in four hours?" Laura said through a clenched jaw.

There was a pause on the other end as the recipient considered bringing in their supervisor. Until now, Laura had been civil, but there was potential to escalate.

"We have calls all over the city," the operator repeated. "We'll send someone as soon as we can, Miss."

Tears streamed down Laura's cheeks. This day was getting worse by the second, and their scripted responses were doing nothing to appease her. It did not help that she had yet to see another vehicle pass by. Being alone and isolated in this part of the city was not doing her any favours.

She wiped her face and sniffled. The ability to breathe clearly, if only for a moment, helped her to focus. Short of going out there and installing the spare herself, Laura was fresh out of options. *Knowing my luck, I'd end up chasing the spare tyre rolling down the street and lose it in a culvert.*

Laura took a deep breath before making one last plea, "Is there anything you can do to speed things up? I'm alone out here, in an unfamiliar neighbourhood…"

Off in the distance, between two large warehouses, there was a sign that lit up the night sky. Since the water running down the glass was distorting her view, she lowered the window long enough to read the sign.

"There's a bar here?" Laura asked herself at a near whisper.

"Miss?" the operator asked.

"Sorry? Nothing," Laura replied. "You'll call to inform me when you send a truck out?"

"Of course—" the operator said.

Focused on that sign, Laura said, "Thank you," and hung up.

She closed the window, removed the key from the ignition, and zipped up her coat. Her clothes were still damp, and her coat would do little to deter the driving rain. However, if she was going to have to wait hours for a truck, she may as well do it with a stiff drink in hand.

"Fuck," Laura said as soon as the door was opened.

Within five steps, her toes were sloshing in water. By the time she reached the end of the alley, she was soaked from head to toe. If the bar was closed, Laura would have to return to her car, start the engine, and crank up the heat just to keep hypothermia from setting in.

To her left, there was an overhang with a muscular well-dressed man standing at the door. His suit was tailored and was probably worth more than everything she had in her closet. Laura paused before realising that her indecision would not get her inside.

"Now or never," Laura said before approaching.

"Can I help you?" the bouncer asked.

She was taken aback by the lack of emotion in that voice. She supposed it would be just as jarring for him to have a lone woman appearing from nowhere in this weather. Still, the water dripping off the tip of her nose served as a reminder to get over her anxiety.

"I have a f-flat t-tyre," Laura said. She spoke up as he raised his hand, "They are going t-to send a t-tow t-truck in s-s-several hours, and I could *r-r-really* use a drink."

The man smiled, the sort of sickly smile she associated with Hollywood psychopaths. Gazing into those dead eyes sent a shiver down her spine. Meanwhile, the man reached for an earpiece and appeared to be listening intently to what was being said.

"You're welcome to wait inside," the bouncer said.

"T-t-thank y-y-you," Laura said, through chattering teeth.

He stepped aside and opened the door. Laura half-expected to hear a jukebox playing rock, blues, or even country western. Instead, she was greeted by a serenade of violins instead. The choice of music soothed her soul. It dispelled any notions that walking into a seedy bar, wet and vulnerable, would be like ringing the dinner bell.

She walked on through the doors and was faced by a narrow corridor that went left thirty paces down the line. On her right there was a window that opened up into a coat check.

"You must be frozen," a girl said.

Laura turned toward the booth and spotted a teenage girl at the coat check. Just like the bouncer, this one was impeccably dressed in a black-and-white uniform. Those eyes twinkled with experience and wisdom. Affixed to a black formal vest was the name '*Hazel.*'

"I am-m-m," Laura said.

"Shall I take your coat and purse?" Hazel asked.

She unzipped her coat and handed it over to Hazel, but kept her purse in hand.

"Why don't you dry off in the bathroom," Hazel said without missing a beat.

"R-r-really?" Laura asked. *It'll give me a chance to freshen up.*

The young woman reached back for a hanger, removed a medallion, and placed them neatly on the counter.

"You'll need this later," Hazel replied. "The ladies' room is to the left of the bar."

"T-thanks," Laura said.

"Anytime," Hazel replied, before adopting a smile reminiscent of the bouncer.

Laura peered down the corner. This place did not line up with her idea of a bar. From here, a bunch of heads were visible. As she walked closer, she realised the guests were seated at round tables covered in white tablecloths, blue napkins, and crystal candleholders.

"The red wine is popular tonight," Laura noted.

Compared to the guests of this place, Laura was a fish out of water. Not only for her being soaking wet, but because of her attire. The women here were dressed in formal gowns, adorned in expensive jewellery and hats. Whereas the men wore expensive suits or tuxedos. *All that's missing is the scent of fine cigars and cognac.*

In comparison, Laura was wearing simple shoes, black stockings, a blue jean skirt, and a white blouse. If she had not been wearing a bra, she would give them an eyeful. Fortunately, her bra and blouse matched tonight. *Even the staff are better dressed than I am.*

Upon reaching the main room, Laura realised this was the upper platform. Including the ground floor, there were three levels with stairs fitted in the middle. They all had a thin row of tables nearest to what appeared to be a dance floor. There was nothing on the lowest level, save a grand piano at its centre with seating for a band at the far end from the entrance. This entire setup evoked scenes from black-and-white movies at some cabaret.

"You'd think I'd been driving in a DeLorean," Laura whispered.

On the top platform, to her left, was a bar that took up the entire wall. Servers dressed similarly to Hazel were travelling in and out of a door located to the right of the bar. She followed the wall and found a hallway. That's when she realised the hallway leading into the club had an incline, because she was effectively going underneath the main entrance.

The first door she came across was the ladies' room. Once Laura opened the door, she was surprised by a uniformed attendant standing there.

"You look like you need to dry off," said the woman with a name tag that said '*Agnes*.'

"That would be great," Laura answered, luxuriating in the heat.

"Here," Agnes said, handing over a stack of hand towels. "Dry off in the stall over there. You're in luck. The show is about to begin."

"Show?" Laura asked.

Agnes nodded curtly. "It's not every day that we get to see one of our *own* perform."

"Who's that?" Laura asked.

"You'll see," Agnes replied cryptically.

Laura stepped into the stall and stripped down, grateful that the towels were warm. She wrung out her clothes before drying herself off. Her nipples were hard from the cold, but the warmth of the towels felt good against her skin. As violin music filtered through the speakers, she closed her eyes, doing her best to excise all those memories from the day she had. Laura took her time drying off.

"Shit," Laura whispered.

She noticed the mess but was marginally successful in cleaning up after herself. Agnes did not seem to mind. The attendant kept on smiling, but Laura's face became flush with blood.

"Now for the hair," Laura whispered.

From out of her purse came a brush, and after digging around a bit, she found an elastic that was not broken or stretched out of shape. Flipping her head over, Laura brushed out her hair and quickly wrapped it into a bun.

"Mind if I remove my makeup?" Laura asked.

"Go ahead," Agnes said.

On any given day, Laura wore little makeup. The mirror confirmed that today's events had taken their toll. She used a fresh towel to wash the makeup smeared from the rain.

She pulled a small makeup bag out of her purse. There was nothing there that would put her in the same league as the women beyond this door. Outside of hitting a few pubs with friends, she rarely went out. Laura hummed along to the music playing in the background, while applying makeup to conceal the bags under her eyes and adding definition to her lashes.

After applying lip gloss for a bit of shine, Laura stepped back and reviewed her *transformation*. To be honest, she remembered looking worse after putting in a lot more effort. Given her situation, this was the best she could do.

"Thank you," Laura said.

A friend of hers once mentioned the associated customs of such bathrooms. To *properly* thank Agnes, she fished out a ten-dollar bill for a tip.

"Keep it," Agnes said. "Club policy."

"Oh," Laura said, "thanks again." *Why do I feel like that's a polite way of telling me that ten dollars isn't worth her time?*

* * *

"What will it be?" the bartender with a name tag that read '*Eugene*' asked.

"Whiskey, neat," Laura said.

"You got it," Eugene replied.

Laura turned around on her stool while Eugene was busy. So far, no one was on the scene, nor were any of the overhead lights projecting onto the piano. She took in the atmosphere, in awe that such a place existed. *I wonder why my friends never mentioned this place?*

Zzzzzt. Zzzzzt.

Her phone vibrated on the bar. She turned around to grab it just as Eugene filled her drink. After the day she had, Laura had no qualms about downing the amber-coloured liquid in one gulp. She tapped her glass against the bar, and he filled it up again.

"Thanks," Laura said.

As a warming sensation overtook her, Laura was ready to look at her phone. She hoped it was something from the towing company, but instead, it was a bunch of emails. Her phone must have connected to this club's open access point while she *freshened* up.

"Great…" Laura whispered.

"Tough day?" Eugene asked.

"That's the understatement of the century," Laura said.

"Really?" Eugene asked, with a hint of interest hanging on that word, daring her to go on.

Laura sighed and looked past Eugene to the mirror. It created the impression that the club was much bigger than it was, because all those tables and lights were reflected. She then focused on her blue eyes and realised that she would not measure up tonight. *Still, it's better than waiting in my car...*

"Stubbed my toe, ruined my stockings, burned my tongue in the first hour," Laura said.

"Not a great start," Eugene confirmed.

"No," Laura said. "That's just the tip of the iceberg."

Laura finished the contents of her drink, and Eugene dutifully filled her glass again.

"Got a call from my cheating husband that he was leaving me," Laura said. "The bastard had a love nest, mistress included, in a trendy part of the city. I spent months with my lawyer lining things up to serve him with divorce papers."

"Why wait?" Eugene said.

"I knew he was hiding something...other than his affair," Laura said. "The bastard claimed we were house poor, and most of my paycheck was going toward the mortgage, utilities, and food."

"So, how did he afford the love nest?" Eugene asked.

Laura finished another drink. This was her third, and she had to slow down or be forced to take a cab. *Why didn't I think of that before?*

"Exactly," Laura said. "My lawyer wanted us to strike first. Use that as justification to freeze his accounts for a forensic audit."

"Didn't—" Eugene said.

The room went quiet as voices turned to whispers. There came a loud click, followed by a flash as a spotlight came to life. Once her eyes adjusted, she spotted a sultry brunette in a formal black dress walking towards the piano.

"I love her!" Laura exclaimed.

"You know the Siren?" Eugene asked in a hushed voice to set the example.

"I first saw her in concert years back," Laura whispered after swivelling toward the bartender. "I didn't know what to expect, but I watched her walk across the stage barefoot. She had this beautiful red dress on that immediately caught my eye. At that moment, I knew it was going to be a night to remember."

"She really made an impression, eh?" Eugene asked.

In the background, the Siren played. Laura's heart sank the moment she realised it was *that* song on the radio from earlier. *On the bright side, I won't hear it again tonight.*

"I've been a fan ever since," Laura said. "Must have seen the Siren in concert a half-a-dozen times so far."

"So, lucky seven then?" Eugene asked.

"I guess—" Laura said.

Zzzzzt. Zzzzzt.

She reached for her phone, and her eyes widened noticeably. It was an email from her lawyer, Emily. The one who called shortly after getting the call from her bastard husband. Emily explained she had no choice but to drop her as a client on account of a conflict of interest.

Even the Siren's haunting voice, the one that often brought her to tears, did not soothe her soul. Her lawyer had left her on account of being involved with the '*other woman.*' It seemed that her husband's lover was left wanting and had been cruising the singles' bars in between visits. *She's not the only one he failed to satisfy.* To add insult to injury, she sent her a bill for services owed.

"Fucking bloodsuckers!" Laura said.

The room went quiet, dead quiet. This time she could hear her own heart beating and blood coursing through her veins.

"Something wrong?" the Siren asked.

Laura looked up from her phone and spotted those green eyes and the natural curls of that black hair. Her jaw dropped as she wondered how she got here so fast.

"I…er…I'm sorry," Laura said. "I've had a bad day—"

"You have a problem with bloodsuckers?" the Siren asked.

"Only…er…what?" Laura asked.

Laura downed another dose of liquid courage, but Eugene did not refill the drink. That's when she caught sight of the tips of fangs sticking out from those beautiful lips. *That can't be…*

"I asked if you had a problem with bloodsuckers," the Siren repeated, giving her a view of those distinctive fangs.

Laura looked at Eugene for help but realised fangs were protruding from his lips as well. Just beyond, she peered at the mirror, momentarily confused, until the last piece fell into place. She was the only one reflected in the mirror.

"I was talking about my lawyer," Laura flubbed, hoping to defuse this situation.

"Oh, we have plenty of those in the room," the Siren said.

The Siren smiled, hummed some haunting tune, and covered the space between them in the blink of an eye. She ran her hands up Laura's bare arms, turning them to gooseflesh. Laura shivered, but did not resist, even as the Siren kissed her neck.

"We aren't all that bad really," the Siren said.

There was something in that voice that left Laura completely disarmed.

"Here," the Siren added. "I'll help you forget your day."

Laura felt a light pinch on her neck and her pupils immediately dilated. She moaned as ecstasy built up like gas thrown on an open flame. Laura came not once, nor twice, but thrice. Each one washed over her like waves in a storm.

"See," the Siren teased. "Isn't that better?"

"More…" Laura whispered.

Her conscious mind was unaware that she was asking for more. As alarm bells went off in her head, warning her of the danger, those thoughts were soon drowned out by her sense of overwhelming need.

"Are you sure?" the Siren asked, taunting with every syllable.

"Yes…" Laura replied, ignoring that faint voice in the back of her mind urging her to wake up from this nightmare.

"Well…" the Siren said. "If you insist."

This time there was no pain, simply an overwhelming burst of pleasure. Laura lost count of the amount of times she orgasmed. This was a first for her, since she was lucky enough to manage one. She *wanted* more. Laura felt her heart rate rise, and she gasped for air. She *needed* more. With one last burst of pleasure, Laura tilted her head back and moaned as her heart faltered and stopped entirely. *What a great day!*

ABOUT THE AUTHOR

Evelyn Chartres is the nom de plume for a self-published Canadian author. The writer of seven Gothic fantasy novels, Evelyn released her debut novel, The Portrait, in 2016, and her latest, Dark Hearts, in 2022.

A fan of the phrase "live to eat," Evelyn shares her recipes on this website. These recipes have a loose focus on French-Canadian cuisine, which feature deep-dish meat pies, seafood, and desserts that are rarely seen outside of La Belle Province.

Evelyn is currently living in Halifax, Nova Scotia, and is busy laying the foundations for her next book featuring Clara Grey.

Small Town Pack

Kayla Hicks

Strange new town, strange new house, and a strange new me.

With each box I'd packed as I'd prepared to move, it was as if I were packing a piece of my old self. And now here I was, on a neatly trimmed street, with new possibilities ahead of me.

Who would have thought that a move to this small town in Virginia was exactly what I needed? Big Stone Gap, a town nestled in the center of the changing fall foliage of a thriving forest.

When I set the last of the boxes inside the small foyer, I looked around the old hardwood floors, white wainscoting walls, and baby blue painted accents on the walls. The small home was quaint and inviting and just what a single girl like me could use in the next stage of my life phase.

Finding out your fiancé was having an affair with both of your best friends tends to shrink your world instantly. Having no other family of my own, I'd decided to leave the city I loved so much and find my own fresh start.

A sharp knock on the large oak door pulled my attention away from the unpacking in my small white kitchen.

Pulling my long blonde hair up into a ponytail, I wiped my forehead of any excess sweat before greeting my visitor.

As the door swung open, a tall man with broad shoulders, a crisp suit, and bright white smile greeted me on my small doorstep.

"Hello," I said, shifting between my feet.

"Hello there," the attractive man said, his words entangled with an accent I couldn't place. "My name is Gunther Worthington and I'm the mayor. And you are?"

"Oh, I wasn't aware I'd be meeting the mayor on my first day here or at all," I stammered, a small laugh escaping me. "My name is Samantha Green."

"Yes, this is how small towns are. Tightly knit and friendly," he said with a grin. "Do you come from a city?"

"New York City."

"Well, we may not be as fancy as the New York you're used to, but I promise that here in Big Stone Gap, we hold our own charm and hidden treasures. For instance, on a good night, you can see every star over in Powell Valley."

"I'll be sure to check that out. Thank you for stopping by."

"Yes, if you should need anything, please feel free to reach out. As Mayor, I'm obligated to take care of all the town's civilians."

Nodding in response, I offered a small wave, closing the door.

I guess my new start would happen sooner than I'd imagined.

* * *

After a long night of unpacking, I decided it was time to see what Big Stone Gap had to offer me.

The small town was a mixture of brick sidewalks and pavement, sweet small businesses and twinkling lights which highlighted the fall backdrop.

Although it didn't take long to walk the stretch of the main street, a small café caught my eye.

Upon stepping through the front door, the smell of coffee and fresh pastries caused my stomach to growl.

"Welcome! How can I help you?" someone from the counter called out.

Turning my attention towards the counter, I came face to face with a woman, her brown hair scooped into a ponytail and her round framed black glasses smudged with something white on the corner.

"Uh, I may need a moment. I haven't had time to look over the menu."

"Oh! Are you the new girl that moved in on Roosevelt Avenue?" the woman asked. "The mayor stopped in yesterday and told us about you."

"News travels fast here," I commented.

"So, you're from the city? That explains why you're gorgeous. Using all of the newest fashion trends!"

"You're too kind," I said nervously, my hand automatically smoothing the hem of my dress.

"I would highly recommend our pumpkin spice latte and our new strawberry pastries. They are just perfect."

"Sure. Thanks for the suggestion. How much?" I asked, pulling out my wallet.

"Don't worry about it. First one is on the house for newcomers," she said with a wave of her hand.

"That's awfully kind of you," I said. "But doesn't that hurt your business when tourists come to visit?"

"You would think, but tourists that visit typically don't want to leave, so I eventually get the money back later," she said, placing my order in front of me. "Here you go."

"Thank you. Can I ask you something?"

She nodded, wiping her hands on her apron.

"Is there anywhere in town hiring?" I asked. "When I moved here, it wasn't exactly planned."

She leaned down to rest her elbows on the counter, one palm under her chin. "You know what? You may be in luck. I think there are some openings around town. We had some people unexpectedly leave town last month. What skills do you have?"

"I worked as a desk clerk for a while, I'm good with numbers, and I'm a fast typer. But I need something that can pay the bills."

"I think there are some openings at the mayor's office for a secretary and at the local furniture store," she said with a smile.

After thanking her, I took my order and headed back out to the picturesque street, which was steadily becoming busier.

Maybe I should have asked for a map.

Despite not knowing a single person, I was greeted by several friendly looking townsfolk as I walked down the street, smiles plastered on their faces.

The first job opportunity that appeared was the furniture shop. As I approached the front of the store, the entire building drew my eye upward, the storefront reaching up three stories. Each floor containing large bay windows with their furniture on display.

Someone was in front of the wooden front door with a frosted glass window embedded in the frame, flipping the closed sign to open.

"Hello there," I greeted. "I heard you were looking to hire someone. I'm new to town."

"Yes, we are," the gentlemen said.

Now closer to him, I could see his red flannel shirt, untucked from his jeans, paired with some hiking boots.

"I'm looking for someone to oversee the books," he continued. "Are you good with numbers?"

"I am. I have desk clerk and managerial experience from a boutique store back in New York City," I explained.

"Ah yes, I see you are the Samantha Green the mayor talked about," he said, peering at me over the brim of his reading glasses. "Come in and I'll show you what you will be working with."

"Oh, should we schedule an interview?" I asked, suddenly feeling nervous and unprepared.

"We're doing an interview right now. I need the help desperately."

Stepping into his shop, I was greeted with warm lighting and dark wood colors. The smell of pine fresh in the air.

"Wow, your shop is beautiful!" I exclaimed.

"Thank you. A business passed down through generations."

Following him through the first floor of the store, we passed several staged sceneries, our feet thudding against the dark hardwood floors.

"Step into my office," he said, gesturing towards an emerald green arm-chair. "My name is Jed, and I've lived in this town my whole life. I'm a big believer in small businesses and I need this business to keep thriving. The truth is, my last bookkeeper left—unexpectedly. And with business being on the up and up, I need someone to help me keep up."

"I see."

"If you could look over these numbers, I'd appreciate it if you could tell me what you think," he explained, sliding a paper across the table.

Scanning the paperwork before me, I could see that he needed to set up an order time frame schedule. This was the only solution to keep up with demand.

"Do you have an order structure set up?" I asked. "A timeline that ranges from point of order to the point the customer receives the order?"

"No…" he said, raising an eyebrow and leaning back.

"If this was put into place, you could set up a schedule for your orders. This would allow you to know the income you can expect and keep you on schedule. Who is your supplier so we can get them on board?"

"You're talking to him."

"You?"

"As I said. Small business. I make all of these pieces myself."

"That is amazing!"

"Samantha, I like you," Jed said, sitting a little straighter. "Can you start today?"

"Yes! Absolutely! Thank you so much. You won't be disappointed."

"Great, let me show you where you'll be working."

Jed led me to a small office in the back of the store that sat directly next to a workshop.

"If the noise bothers you, let me know. But I try to do most of my work early in the morning before the store opens," Jed explained.

Nodding, I sat down at the cluttered desk and began sifting through the piles.

"Well, I'll leave you to it."

Things are going way too well for me.

* * *

Hours later.

"Still working in here?" Jed asked from the doorway. "I see you've made progress."

"Yes. I've organized all your orders and transactions for you. I also placed a timeline on the computer that you can access. It allows you to update the progress of your orders as you go."

"Is that so?" he asked, his expression showing shock. "Well, you may be the best decision I've made in a long time."

"Thanks."

"But I should let you go for the night. See you in the morning Samantha, bright and early," he said.

"Sounds good," I said, stretching my arms out in front of me. "I'm actually going to take the mayor's advice and do some stargazing over at Powell's Valley tonight."

Jed's expression quickly changed from friendly to uncomfortable. "It's a full moon tonight, so you may not see many stars. Later in the week will work better for stargazing."

"Oh, well, at least living here I can go out there as often as I'd like," I said with a smile, standing up from my chair.

"Please be careful, Samantha. I know that you're used to city life, but these parts have wildlife you aren't prepared for. *Bears, wolves, coyotes. And tonight is perfect hunting weather.*"

"Thank you, I will be."

* * *

Now surrounded by the darkness, I stepped through the soft, lush grass of Powell Valley.

The rolling hills around me created the illusion that I was in a dark ocean, the brilliant backdrop being the starry skyline and the brilliant full moon.

The Autumn chill was settling in now, my breaths coming out in small puffs of clouds in front of me as I walked along.

After spotting the perfect spot near the tree line at the tallest hill, I laid out my blanket, getting myself settled. And once I'd gotten comfortable, it was easy to see what the mayor had been talking about. The entire sky was enveloped in stars except for the lighter circumference of sky surrounding the moon's bright light.

Leaning backward, I placed a blanket beneath my head and allowed myself to relax.

Even from here, I could see the town of Big Stone Gap nestled quietly in the crook of two towering hills covered in forest. The lights in the buildings steadily being turned off as the sleepy quaint town began to slumber.

Turning my attention back to the sky, I heard the rustling of leaves behind me in the forest as a breeze blew by.

My mind wandered back to what Jed had mentioned earlier. Bears, wolves, coyotes. And tonight is perfect hunting weather.

Louder and more consistent leaf rustling began to sound from the woods behind me, causing my heart to race.

Sitting up quickly, I spun around, my eyes scanning the shadows between the trees behind me.

Slowly, I inched backward as a golden and orange-colored leaf pile moved, my breath catching mid-breath.

I'm imagining things.

Forcing myself to relax, a small grey squirrel suddenly pounced out from the leaf pile, running across my blanket and up my arm before it leapt into the clearing, scurrying out of sight.

"Just a squirrel, Samantha," I said aloud, my heart pounding from the sudden exertion.

Another crunch of leaves sounded from the woods, causing me to laugh at my own fears.

Seeing that my blanket was now scrunched and folded, I smoothed out the corners, trying to recreate the previously serene moment.

When a low guttural growl sounded to my right, my heart stopped completely.

As if in slow motion, a large brown wolf pounced from the darkness, landing on top of me, pinning me to the ground. Instinctively, I shielded my face with my forearms as the wolf's teeth latched onto me, quickly piercing my coat, and making contact with my skin.

Crying out in pain, I kicked and screamed with everything in me, trying to get the beast to release me.

However, the wolf's large jaws held firm, its eyes staring straight into my own as low growls erupted once more from deep in its chest.

"Get the fuck off of me!" I yelled, kicking my boot upward high enough to waver the balance it had on its hind legs.

But despite weakening its balance, it remained steady in its mission to hunt me, never letting go of my arms, causing us to roll together down the hill into the valley below.

Dizzy and disoriented, I kicked my feet towards the beast, my screams coming in jagged gasps now.

As a loud growl began to build within the beast, however, a brown blur of fur leapt toward my assailant, detaching him from me.

Without a second thought, I painfully crawled until I was able to stand and began sprinting towards the town when I saw several other wolves sprinting towards me head on. Panic rising like bile in my throat, I pivoted and began sprinting towards the forest.

I need to find a tree to climb.

Dodging tree after tree in the dark forest, I stumbled over rocks and protruding tree roots as my gaze searched desperately for a ray of hope.

A large tree a few yards in was the answer, two low branches reaching out to me.

"Samantha! Run!" Jed's voice echoed.

The fear thick in his tone ignited my own fear like never before, my body leaping toward the lowest branch.

As my hands caught hold, the wounds on my forearms streamed blood down my arms and began soaking my shirt, the pain of my wounds now almost unimaginable.

"Samantha, I'm sorry it came to this," said a voice with a familiar accent.

The mayor.

"If you had just waited another night to come out and star gaze, you too could have joined the pack," the mayor's voice said from somewhere behind me. "Wolves always travel in packs. And everyone in this town is part of the pack."

"Please, just let me go!" I begged, my arms giving out and dropping me to the now wet ground below.

"I wish I could, Samantha. I actually held out hope for you," the mayor's voice said from the darkness. "Something I hadn't felt in a long time. You even won over Jed, the oldest member of the pack. Poor fellow didn't make it either."

Sobs now escaped me, knowing my fate was sealed. Nothing was going to save me now.

"Get her," the mayor's voice now came in a growl.

ABOUT THE AUTHOR

Kayla Hicks is mostly known for The Backup Superhero series, but she is a multi-genre author with works also in Young Adult Dystopian, Contemporary Romance, Horror, and Children's literature.

To find out more about Kayla Hicks visit: kayla-hicks.com/

Other

Rose J Fairchild

You know We exist, yet you deny Us. Ancients. That wild otherness. The unknown. We are one energy with many faces—the tentacles that feed the Whole.

You deny Us, because you're afraid. And you should be. We can do anything to anyone at any time. We created you, after all. Your galaxy, your world, all birthed because of Us.

We are infinite and all-knowing, yet you think you can outwit Us—even control Us. It amuses Us, so sometimes, We let you.

Since We know this is too much for your human mind to process, We'll break it down for you. A single tentacle sliding into your world. Forget the other threads, and don't even try to imagine the Whole.

Here I am now, a single drop in the massive pool of Other. Something different, distinct, and previously unknown to you. That's how you define Us, right?

We appear to you in infinite ways, under many names. Fae, aliens, cryptids, gods, demons, angels, and so much more. But there I go overwhelming you again. To make this easier for you, I need to pick a face.

I'll be female, because humans see women as safe, weak, and innocent. They'd never hurt anyone, right? Except We know better.

Sorry, *I* know better.

Females are closer to Us than males could ever be. Gentle and alluring, they radiate all that is good, the fierceness beneath hidden from the world, and sometimes, even themselves. This is both a blessing and a curse, but you already know that.

And I won't go into their intelligence, strength and sheer determination. The way they can make something from nothing, or heal with a simple touch. No, not today. And I won't tell you We favor them. I won't tell you, but…well, let's move on.

I gather my energy, forming a deceptively curvy form. It's soft, hiding muscle and sinew designed to bend and stretch. To survive. For now, I am devoid of features. A gorgeous walking shadow of stars and midnight.

What else do I need?

Let's go with…pale skin, and wide, gray eyes. A cascade of long, blonde hair. Many humans would mistake this form as non-threatening. Simple, even. But since you're with me, you know better. And if you don't, well, there's less hope for your race than We thought.

Do you see why you amuse Us? The assumptions you make because of an appearance? A gender? Ridiculous, but so easy to manipulate.

The outfit now. I want to play, but not work too hard. So…a sheer, frothy blouse over a white tank top.

No bra. I hate those things. Anyone who's had the misfortune of wearing one of those for a few hours can attest to how strong women are.

Next, a short, hunter-green skirt, paired with matching stiletto heels, and the outfit is complete.

The hair gets a bit of a wave, the eyelids, some shimmer. Rosy cheeks, dewy lips, and now we're in business.

Ready to hunt? I'm hungry.

Come, come. Don't be shy. We're going to the city streets, where prey abounds.

Which city? Doesn't matter, unless you dislike a particular kind of food. Like anything else, humans taste like what they consume. I usually pop into wherever calls to me.

You won't be eating? Oh, good. More for me.

We've arrived. Can you smell it? The twist of fear and excitement? The thick, sticky sadness and the sharp bite of overconfidence born of anonymity? That last one is what We're relying on tonight, my friend.

You can't smell those things? You smell pizza, fried things, and coffee? True. You can find those in abundance here.

And one can always detect exhaust, wood chips, beer, rotting trash, and I'm pretty sure that garbage can has urine on it.

Oh, yes, there's a bar. Definitely urine. That also means We're on good hunting grounds.

Don't crowd me. You'll blow my cover as the lost, lonely female. Just sit back and watch a pro work. It'll all be over soon.

I sway and lean back against the bar's brick wall, breathing in the stench of stale alcohol. I let the swells of my chest rise and fall, thrilled by the way they catch the rainbow of glaring neon lights. I run a finger over them, tracing the colors. Let my head drop back against the wall, mouth slack, as though intoxicated.

Just that fast, I've caught a man's interest. Several, actually. But only one is bold enough to hold my gaze when I turn his way. I smile. Bite my lip. Run one finger down my chest, pulling the tank top lower. I pretend not to notice I'm almost falling out of it.

Music pulses through me—an electric thrill of pleasure. I snake my hips in a little dance and throw the lanky, dark-haired man a saucy look. He steps toward me and I push off the wall, dancing toward him. With a well-placed step, I snap a heel, falling neatly into his arms.

"Ouch!"

He catches me. Draws me close. "You okay?"

I turn my face upward, meeting his stare, and let my words slur. "Yeah, thanks to you." I lift a hand and poke the end of his nose with my forefinger.

With a laugh, the man allows his gaze to slip lower, drinking in my overflowing cleavage. "You, uh…want a drink?"

"You don't have to do that!" I laugh and bite my lip again. I can smell his eagerness. "I should probably go home, anyway." But I know he won't let me leave.

"Nah, you're good. Just took a little tumble is all. Listen, there's a spot in the back here where you can kick off your shoes and sit. The chairs are comfy, too. In fact, why don't you take those busted things off right here, and

I'll give you a piggyback ride to my table?"

My hero. I kick off the broken one first, then the other. He backs up to me.

"Put your arms around my neck, okay?"

Don't mind if I do. What? You know what I came here for. But you're right. It's not time yet.

I wrap them loosely over his shoulders. Reaching down to his chest, I give his pectorals a gentle rub. I'm pressed against his back, heat building between us. He smells like rum and sugar.

His muscles stiffen. Other things, too. I hear him swallow, choke, and clear his throat as his pulse ramps up. "Now, just hop up and wrap your legs around my waist. I'll catch you."

I smirk, then do as I'm told with a little jump. He keeps his word, catching my bare thighs in his grip. I lay my chin on his shoulder, breath caressing his ear, his five o'clock shadow scraping my cheek. He slides his hands toward my barely covered backside. Rough fingers graze me, and he sucks in a breath as he discovers I've forgotten underwear.

And you! Don't think I've forgotten about you. Come along, or you'll miss the fun.

We enter the bar. The music washes over me, as I take in the lights and glittering glass beneath them. It smells delicious here. Aside from the creations of an obviously talented chef, seduction and temptation permeate the room, lacing the air with a salted caramel thickness that clings to the skin and coats the tongue.

People sit at tables in an odd, half-poisoned courtship dance. Well, some of them do. Some are here with friends. It's easy to tell those ones. They laugh louder and speak openly. No posturing necessary.

My prey carries me to a small table littered with an almost empty plate of shellfish, and a half-full glass of something dark. He dips down, allowing me to slide off his back, then helps me to my seat.

I leave my skirt high, delighting in the cool air on my warmer parts. His gaze drifts low, sending his heartbeat into a gallop. I open my legs slightly. Enough to tease, but not enough for a better view. It does the trick, though.

Do you see how he leans closer? Can you hear the frantic beating of his heart? Smell the excitement dripping from him? See the rise and fall of blood at his pulse points?

I can. And now I'm starving.

Are you sure you don't want some? He's ripe with need, and pickled in alcohol to boot. Aren't humans supposed to like pickles?

Fine. I'll devour him all on my own, then. And soon. I don't think I can wait much longer.

I glance at the seafood, and somehow, he's able to pull his eyes away from the prize long enough to notice. I continue to stare at it, lip curling in displeasure. "Oh. Are you allergic to shellfish?" he asks.

I chuckle. "Thankfully, no."

"Hungry, then?"

"You have no idea how much."

Standing, he says, "I'll get you something to eat. What are you hungry for?"

"You."

His throat bobs around a swallow. "Forward. I like it. But let's have a drink first. Get to know each other a little bit. Wine okay?" I nod and he goes to fetch it.

I feel you judging me. You think he might be a good guy, right? Do I need to remind you of the finger-grazing incident? That wasn't accidental.

He's just human, you say? Exactly. So he's flawed by nature, and perfectly edible.

I'm handed a glass of ruby wine, and smile at my morsel as he returns to the seat across from me. I dip my finger in the wine, lick the glistening tip. He gulps, almost loud enough to echo. Or so it seems to me.

Stop being so squeamish. It's just a finger. Focus!

Now, where was I? Oh, yes. Waiting for him to give in to his own hunger.

Sipping his drink, he studies me, allowing his eyes to rove over my curves. "What's your name?"

Good question. I think of something that sounds delicious—strong and dark, smooth and earthy. "Morgan. And you?"

"That's a beautiful name…Morgan."

It rolls around his mouth. By beautiful, he means it's mysterious and alluring. Like me. I smile, exposing brilliant teeth. He grins back foolishly, not noticing their pointed gleam.

"I'm Jake." Puffing out his chest, he looks every bit the proud peacock when he's more of a turkey, like his namesake.

Reaching across the table, I grab his hand and give it a soft shake. "Nice to meet you, Jake."

He raises his glass. "The pleasure's all mine." Dark liquid tips into his mouth, throat expanding and contracting to allow its passing. I press the tip of my tongue to the point of one canine. Taste blood. But it's my own. Not nearly as satisfying as his will be.

I lift my glass in response. "Cheers." One sip. Two sips. I swig the rest of the glass and he stares at me open-mouthed.

Grinning, I set the glass down too hard, feigning drunkenness. I lift it, pull it close to my eyes as though out of focus, and tilt my head sideways. He thinks I'm inspecting it for damage, but it's all part of the act.

"It's okay. You didn't break it. Do you want another?"

I slide my tongue over my teeth suggestively. "No. I want you."

He almost drops his glass. One more sip and he sets it down on the table, swallowing hard. "I want you, too."

"Right now."

Glancing around, he leans close to me and whispers, "Where did you have in mind?"

Standing, I trap his hand in mine, pulling him toward the door. He tosses cash on the table and follows me out like a lost puppy.

Showtime. Let's go, my friend, and soon you'll see what We can do.

Dropping his hand, I skip ahead of him, turning down an alley. Then another. I hear him behind me, and you behind him.

"Hey, wait up!"

"Come. I'm ready for you." I choose my words carefully. They have power, and you'd do well to remember that.

I duck behind some hedges outside of an office building.

"Where are you?" His voice is husky with secret cravings—so close I can almost taste him.

"In the bushes. I'm waiting…" I let my voice be breathy. Breathless. Even you feel its caress. Shh. It's okay. Our little secret. It's in your nature to want to be desired. Devoured. We made you that way.

He crashes through the foliage, panting.

I point to the ground. "Lie down."

He does. Good boy.

Oh, take off those judgy-pants, will you? He's well-trained. Perfectly eager to listen when he gets the treat at the end. Now, let's find out if he can beg.

Crawling over him, I lace my fingers through his and press his hands above his head. His heart pounds, its vibrations singing against my flesh. I dip my head and press my lips to his. Open, so he can taste me.

When I pull away, he gasps. "I want to touch you."

"No, naughty boy. You have to earn that privilege."

Grinning, I feel his hips rise, grinding against me. "Sure, Morgan. What do you want me to do?"

I let the thrill of having a name slide over me. Of feeling unique for once.

Yes, even We like to feel special. And what's wrong with that? Why do you think We show up in forms that terrify? That demand respect? It makes Us feel special. Powerful. And now, pulling me from my reverie, is the distant rumble of ancient hunger.

Back to work, then.

I smile. Kiss his neck. "You let me do whatever I want first. Then you'll get your turn."

He shivers. "Yes, ma'am."

I kiss his neck again, then give it a little bite. A tiny nip.

His breaths are short and fast.

The hunger comes again, a clap of thunder across my awareness. It's too much, and I slide lips and teeth over the side of his neck, the pulse of his artery beckoning. I bite, mouth filling with blood as he screams and thrashes beneath me.

"Please! Don't!" Turns out he *can* beg.

I open my jaw wider than humanly possible and clamp down again. His words drown in a wet crunch. silencing his cries. His breath gurgles under my mouth, the flex of soundless words moving against my face.

Skin blanching white, his heart slows…stops. He stills beneath me. I sit up and study his vacant eyes, then close them.

That thunderous hunger rolls through me again. I stand and look at you. Lick blood from my lips.

Did that excite you? Do I? Come to me, my friend. I want to look at you. Hold you.

Taste you.

It never stops, you know. That hunger? It's an ache We can never fill.

But We try.

And you help.

So soft. So easy.

Hush now, my sweet. See how special you are? A sacrifice chosen to feed Us. And with that, you return to Us. Become Us.

The Other.

ABOUT THE AUTHOR

ose J. Fairchild is a Dark Fantasy author who writes stories of blood and beauty, gifting fangs and claws to those who need them most. She juggles writing around family, pets, and a library job in the mysterious Catskill Mountains of Upstate New York where all things magical (and sometimes terrible) live. She's previously had short stories published in anthologies by Fae Corps, Inc., and is currently working on three Dark Fantasy novels.

The Richest Red Velvet

Melissa Rose Rogers

*A*s on every Halloween, Victoriene awoke earlier than any other day of the year. She had been busy preparing for the party that evening for days, but there was still much to be done. The butcher was set to deliver, and the new delivery boy was a little careless. He'd missed one of the blood deliveries last week. It hadn't been a catastrophe, but Victoriene had delved into the stockpile of frozen blood for her sweet treats, and a few customers had commented on the change. Most of her clientele were older and abhorred technology, but there were several outliers—tech-savvy young vamps. A one-star review on the Internet had made her bare her fangs. In her reply, she had apologized for the change in quality and tried to diplomatically word her response so as to not alienate future customers. At least she had her regulars, and few newer vamps were being made per the council.

Victoriene's old heart pounded in anger at the thought that the stupid human might have ruined her plans for the evening. *I don't have time to think about that*, she told herself, rising from her coffin.

Before long, she was dressed and sipping on a bubble tea made with coconut water. *Passable*, she thought. *At least it makes me feel less guilty than human blood. Plus, it's a trendy menu item. A diet of mostly coconut water and stabilized pork blood, and does anyone appreciate it? Why do I even bother?* She knew without thinking the words to herself: guilt over subsisting off humans was why.

She sauntered downstairs from her apartment to the coffee shop kitchen, slipped her black chef's jacket over her corset, and placed the chef's hat over her abundant platinum curls. The fluorescent lights buzzing was the only sound to accompany her thoughts. For tonight's party, she would need to prepare the Jack-o'-lantern drinks, and the Apricot Sunray punch. First, she needed to take care of the longest prep times. She preheated the oven for the frozen mac 'n' cheese cups, mini quiches, and other hors-d'oeuvre for the humans, then set to work filling prep bowls for the red velvet cake. Her recipe used stabilized pig's blood instead of eggs, an old trick giving the cake a more satisfying flavor with the added heme. *I hope that delivery boy gets here soon.* She sighed, looking at the clock. *The contracted waitstaff should also arrive just after sundown.* They were newer vamps, all recommended by the coven, but she didn't know them well.

The bells on the front door clanged. Victoriene looked up. An unfamiliar human scent tugged at her. She set down the flour container next to the scale. *Tiffany must have forgotten to lock up earlier. I'll have to speak to her about that,* thought Victoriene. Tiffany, a human twenty-something, was ignorant of vampires' existence but was an excellent barista and more than capable of ringing up a book. Not that many humans came here for the books. It was a strange, claustrophobic collection with an organization that made sense only to Victoriene, who admittedly, was born far, far before the Dewey Decimal System had been dreamt up.

Victoriene set timers in the kitchen for two reasons: one to keep the food from burning on this tight schedule, and two so that she had a hard cut off for kicking out whoever had intruded into her store while it was closed.

On the other side of the kitchen doors and past the bar with its polished wood and gleaming machines, were the stacks.

Victoriene breathed in deeply and could smell masculine cologne, and an absence of nonenal—a young man? She pushed through the Jenga towers of books, the bookcases of volumes stacked sideways, making a beeline towards the human.

She bounded the corner to find a man with short hair, a medium complexion, and an average build. His mini-check plaid shirt was tucked into khakis, but instead of preppy, he seemed outdated. She cleared her throat, and he turned to face her. Under his arm was tucked a thick plastic clipboard and on his index finger was a clump of dust scraped off a book cover.

"I hope your kitchen is cleaner than this," he said, raising his brows over thick spectacles with an intensity that made her want to backhand him and hiss. He wiped the dust between his fingers and it drifted to the floor in a gray blob. "Kieran Donnelly, health inspector. And you are?"

"Victoriene, the owner," she said with her upper lip raised as she fought to keep from snarling.

"We haven't met. Usually, I see Tiffany on these inspections." He pulled out the clipboard and produced a pen.

Of course, he'd see Tiffany. I'm not usually awake during business hours, she thought before saying, "it's Halloween. There's a special party tonight, and I'm cooking. Let's get this over with." The control she was demonstrating filled her with a bit of pride. Her younger self might have actually ripped his head off.

The inspector made his way behind the coffee bar, after glancing into the bare display case, emptied to showcase the red velvet cake for the party. He paused over a napkin folded like a bat and glanced at an instruction sheet next to it before moving on. He examined the labels for the appliances. "Good, all commercial grade."

Annoyance was creeping higher and higher within her. He was taking so long to scribble notes on that pad. *What could he possibly be writing?*

He perused the shelves of syrup, the rows of white mugs, the shelves of coffee beans. This was Tiffany's jurisdiction. *She's pretty competent. I shouldn't worry about this,* Victoriene thought as he picked up a bag of beans and flipped it over, expelling the aroma with the motion. She tapped her foot to release some of her tension, but that wasn't really helping. He stared at her foot for a long beat, then moved to the stainless steel mini fridge.

"The apple juice isn't dated," he observed before scribbling on the paper.

"I'll mention that to Tiffany. We go through so much of it, I'm sure it slipped her mind," Victoriene said, sighing.

Kieran turned heel and pushed through the swinging doors into her kitchen. The aroma of the quiches and mac 'n' cheese cups cooking was delightful. Even though she didn't *need* to eat human food, she still enjoyed it from time to time. *I suppose it is what grass would be to humans, something they are capable of consuming but offering no sustenance. At least,* she thought, *human food tastes appetizing. I don't see too many humans chewing the green stuff.*

The plaid wearing man pinched his face together as he opened her commercial fridge. This was her arena, where she was more confident about what he would encounter. The timer for the mac 'n' cheese cups went off. Victoriene swung the oven open and pulled the pan out. Kieran gaped at her in horror. She looked down at her rapidly healing hands. *Oh, that's right. Humans don't have rapid healing. To me, this is no big deal, but it would hurt for him.*

Another timer went off—the mini quiches. This time, she fumbled for a hot pad before retrieving the fragrant pies. Kieran was still watching her with an expression she didn't quite understand. *Not quite set in the middle,* she thought, placing them back in the oven.

He moved from the commercial fridge to her pantry. *I don't have time for this. I need to just start working on the cake.* She greased and floured the pans, and measured all the ingredients into prep bowls, save the missing blood. Flour trailed behind her as she put the container back in the pantry. When she was about to prep the frosting ingredients for the smaller stand mixer, Kieran returned.

"I need to see your dumpster area," he said.

She just pointed toward the back door, before stepping out of the path of any stray sunlight beams, though the sun was setting. She pretended to look for a utensil, but she was on her last nerve. He left the door open, the screened door banging in place while he was outside with his checklist. She was grateful for the north-facing back door and its reduced light.

She stared at the wall clock, wishing it would stop and thought, *I might be preternaturally fast, but good food can't be rushed. Where is the delivery guy? I need that pig's blood.*

Kieran returned, shutting the door behind him, and she selected a small paring knife from the block. Her mind was made up.

"I've had to knock down a few points for employee hygiene," he said, staring at her pointedly. "You should know better than to have unrestrained hair. You should know better than to wear so much jewelry. It might be Halloween, but you still need to practice food safety. Also, there was flour or sugar on the floor. And I don't see the three-step washing station set up, so I can't grade you for that."

Victoriene was seething as she pushed her abundant blonde curls over her shoulders. *This is such a big night for me, and these stupid humans are ruining it.* She kept from muttering aloud as she stepped toward him and pushed into his mind, finding his defining fear: being inherently wrong and bad. She tugged on that fear, first breaking it open into a river, then damming it with herself. The clipboard clattered to the floor. His eyes slackened into a dead cow gaze, caught in her mesmerism. She slit across his wrist, and he paled as blood poured into a measuring cup. When she had enough, she pressed his arm to her lips. It had been a long time since she'd drank from a human, and maybe she'd feel guilty later, but the anger swirling through her was louder than her sympathy. After her anger and hunger subsided, he stood there paralyzed by her mind. She gave him a swallow of black blood from her own wrist, and the wound sealed, leaving only cherry red drops on his warm skin, a few splatters on his khakis, and droplets where she'd dribbled on the floor. She hadn't a moment to lose. She left him, statue-still, as both the frosting and cake whirred into motion.

She considered her to-do list. *Next, I'll work on the blood oranges for the Apricot Sunray punch.*

A buzzer sounded—it was the back door. She carefully swung the door open, revealing not only that the sun had set but also the sloth of a delivery man from the butchers. He shoved a clipboard, cheap and wooden, with a PO form toward her. She signed the order and waited as he hauled in several boxes with bags of blood in them, and sundry pork pieces on the side—bacon, tenderloins, sausage.

He froze as he rounded the door. "Something's burning," he sniffed.

She turned and remembered the mini quiches. She'd been so focused on her cake that she'd forgotten about them. *Another thing ruined by stupid humans*, she thought, sighing. Victoriene rushed over to the oven. Opening the door released a billow of gray smoke and the charred quiches were black as her endless night. She put down the pan, shut off the oven, and tried to think of how she could fix this when she had no time. *It was just one thing after another tonight--the burnt quiches, the late delivery, the obnoxious health inspector. The health inspector.*

Victoriene turned to see the delivery boy poking the unmoving, unblinking health inspector.

"Big yikes. Is this guy stroking out or something?" He looked at Victoriene with a sheepish expression.

"Or something," she replied, closing the distance. She switched off the smaller mixer, hoping she'd not over-mixed the batter. This was another human ruining her special party. She gazed deeply into his eyes, finding his core fear: failure, incompetence. Once the delivery was unloaded, she would have no need of him, so there was no need to keep him frozen.

"You're good at what you do," she beamed into his mind. He repeated this back to her in his own words.

"You'll finish this delivery and forget all about the guy *stroking out*. You'll go back to work. Nothing unusual happened here." She patted him on the cheek. It was better to use their own words back at them than to try to introduce new concepts.

He spurred into motion, just as she realized she had yet another audience, this time invited. It was the vampire waiters. The smoke from the burnt quiches swirled around them and gave the kitchen an otherworldly feel, perfect for Halloween.

"It looks like you've had a messy evening," said one of the predatory figures in black. The vamp was cold, stoic—probably a young one that couldn't handle the complexities of fully living, fully feeling, and so had chosen to stunt itself.

"Humanity was seemingly conspiring against me," she sniffed, "you lot can set up the small plates," she commanded, pointing to white stacks on a stainless steel shelf. "The napkins should be folded like bats. There are instructions and an example behind the coffee bar."

The delivery boy finished unloading, and with a wave left via the back door.

The vampire waiters, too, had spurred into motion, whizzing in and out of the kitchen with the plates. Victoriene sped over to the stand mixers, poured the cake batter into the prepared pans, and set a new timer. *Finally, it's in the oven.* She darted to Kieran's clipboard, pulled off the carbon copied form of her infractions, and scrunched it into a ball. Tossing it in the trash felt very satisfying. She reached again into his mind and quelled the torrent of fear petrifying him.

"Deep down you're deserving: you're worthy," she soothed.

He relaxed and agreed with her in his own words, his voice quaking with relief.

"Fill out a new form," she instructed, "you were clumsy with the last one. We had a near-perfect grade—just an unlabeled apple juice bottle and too much jewelry for me. It's Halloween. You know I just wanted to get a head start on my costume."

He nodded, took the clipboard from her, and began writing again.

Now she needed to whip something up to replace those quiches and quick. *At least the oven's still hot.* She turned on a vent fan for the smoke and then dashed into the cold room and scanned it for frozen morsels. Filo pastries filled with cheese and spinach. *Good enough*, she thought, rushing them to a baking sheet.

When his pen stopped moving, she took hold of Kieran's mind again, forcing him to forget, and go on his way.

"All done with the setup," one of the vampire waiters said as she was setting the cake pans to cool.

"Excellent," Victoriene said, "now we just need to work on the prep for the drinks." She poured herself a cup of punch and took the smallest of sips.

"This needs a bit more ginger ale to balance it, I think."

She motioned toward the storeroom, and one of the black-clothed waitstaff spurred into motion.

"We need more blood oranges sliced up for the Apricot Sunray punch, too."

Calm replaced chaos as she finished readying herself and her establishment for the most important night of the year. The party went off without a hitch, pleasing humans and vampires alike. In the dead of the night, before the humans began filtering out, Victoriene finally felt like she had a chance to just take in the party. The waitstaff had everything under control, so she looked over the partiers, deciding where to mingle. The cake was mostly gone, the appetizers picked over, and the punch nearly drained. Quiet laughter, fangs not hidden, among the vampires was a fresh change from the infighting she'd experienced in her youth. The humans felt comfortable enough to talk and flirt with the vampires—they were safe so long as they were here. Pride filled her in having made it all come together despite the stressors of the evening.

The next evening, Victoriene awoke to an update to her poor Internet review that almost made her tear up:

***** UPDATE: The Richest Red Velvet

I gave this place another try after the owner's response. I figured why not try the special Halloween party? It's been hyped so much, it seemed like the place to be. The boozy Apricot Sunray punch tasted like pure sunlight—it was so fresh and cut the chocolate of the red velvet cake perfectly. The menu had stated that there were artificial flavors for the cake, but nothing about it tasted artificial. The red was vibrant, and it didn't taste of beets or food coloring. It had an almost savory quality to it. The proprietor could have fooled me. It was decadent and deeply satisfying. The atmosphere and wait staff were great. I hope she maintains this level of excellence for all her evening services. I would give it 5 stars but knocked off one for that prior disappointment.

It must have been a young vamp, Victoriene thought. *So self-important.*

* * *

Author's Note: This story was inspired by two memes I saw on Pinterest. One was claiming that coconut water has been used as an alternative to blood plasma in emergencies (kind of true), and another that blood can be used as an egg substitute in baking (true).

Melissa Rose Rogers writes speculative stories and is inspired by mythologies from all over the world. She currently lives in Denver, CO, where she experiments on her husband and daughters with recipes she finds online. She loves board games, memes, and long walks in the dry, thin air. Her fiction appears in Bear Creek Gazette, Tales from the Moonlit Path, 96th of October, Harvey Duckman Presents, Bewildering Stories, and various anthologies.

You can find out more about her at melissaroserogers.com

A Cross and a Girl Named Red

A.C. Merkel

You find yourself sneaking down an alley at night. You're with a girl—no, a woman. She's tall with bronze skin and long, thick, curly black hair. She looks back at you and her smile makes you feel so many things. The biggest thing is lust. You don't remember her, so you dial that back.

She frowns. "You've reset again."

You're confused, but you go with it. "It would seem so. I'm sorry, but I don't remember you."

She looks like she might cry, but she hides it quickly with a caring smile. "Don't worry, we'll find a cure. I'm Meredith. My friends, including you, call me Mer."

"Like the sea," you say, grinning at her.

You see that she is uncomfortable. "I'm sorry, Mer."

"It's not your fault, but we need to press onward." She turns and moves stealthily down the alley. You're watching her, mirroring her steps. Her wild hair and golden skin make you flush with heat. You know in your heart that you already love her. You also know this fact makes her upset. Your thoughts are interrupted by her voice. It's got an edge to it, hardened and focused, as if sneaking down dark alleys is normal.

"Okay, I know you don't remember anything, but this is where you come in. I want you to take a deep breath, and then tell me which way to go."

"How will I—" You don't finish your thought. A smell permeates your nose. Acrid. Different. You smell Mer as well. She smells like lavender and… You change the course of your thoughts, remembering her earlier discomfort. You step forward and extend your hand to her. "This way."

She nods and almost reluctantly takes your hand. You wonder what you did to make things so awkward between the two of you. Maybe you can fix it? As you look down at her hand, you notice your clothes. You're wearing a short plaid skirt, fishnets, and boots. *Doc somethings.* You're also wearing a white tank top and a leather jacket. *Am I Buffy?* You shake your head. You remember a TV show of all things. You'd be happier if you remembered Mer.

The two of you follow the acrid smell, hand in hand, to a tall fence. On the other side is an industrial site. It's populated with barrels, brick buildings, and smokestacks.

You motion with your hands. "Whatever—*whomever?*—we have been following, they are in there."

Meredith nods. She releases your hand and then crouches. With a powerful thrust, she clears the fence, razor wire and all. She turns and motions with her hand. "Come on," she whispers.

You laugh. "I can't do that. Are you a superhero?"

"If I'm a superhero, you are too." Mer grins.

You shrug and copy her deep crouch. You push off, and just like her, you clear the fence by mere inches. As you land, you feel your face change. Your tongue has a sharp pain and your mouth fills with a metallic taste. You touch your face. It's distorted, shifted. It seems more gaunt and sharp. You look at Mer. She looks the same as she had.

She laughs quietly. "You're a vampire."

"Are you—"

"No," she interrupts. "I'm something else. My transition is much more extreme and takes more to bring it on. We should hurry. The monster we're tracking could be hurting someone. Every second we waste…" Her voice trails off.

She turns and you follow, still checking the fangs that blossomed in your mouth and cut your tongue. As you follow the scent, you realize the smell is familiar, like when a tomcat marks his territory. You wonder what other things you remember. Like Buffy. You know where you are: Ohio. This plant belongs to a steel manufacturer. You want to look at Mer again. But she's behind you, so it would be too obvious. You don't know what you did to make her shy away, so how can you make up for it?

You pause at the corner of a building. "We're close."

Mer takes your hand. Hers is warm. Yours seems like ice in comparison. *Right, vampire.*

You act brave, leaning out from the corner to see the path ahead. It runs between two buildings. There's a large fixture hanging over the nearest door. You sniff. "They're inside."

"*They're*, as in *you don't know their gender*, or there's more than one?" Mer asks, now also leaning into the small alley. She presses against your back and you casually take a deep breath. You want to inhale her essence, but you don't wish to cause her any further discomfort.

Instead, you answer. "I think there are at least two distinct scents. They're some kind of human-cat hybrid, right?"

Mer pulls you back into the cover of darkness. "Is that what you smell? Cat people?"

You nod. "Yes, it smells like…well…" You cringe and make a face.

Mer laughs a humorless laugh. "Cat-shifters. This is their territory."

You wonder why it has to be her. Why does she have to track these things in the night? And why does she have to do it with such a useless vampire?

Mer is unphased. "I'm going to peek into the window and see what we're dealing with. Stay here. Be ready to run or fight."

You feel your teeth again. They had relaxed as you snuck through the dark; now, they are back with a vengeance. You try to speak, but it comes out as a mumble. "I think I'm ready."

"What?" Mer asks.

You give a thumbs-up signal. *Stupid teeth.*

Mer leaves you at the corner. You watch as she gracefully slinks across the path and compresses her back against the wall. She's a gorgeous woman. Maybe twenty-some years old. From a distance, you don't get locked into her eyes like you have been since you first saw her. With physical distance, you can see past the whole to notice her clothes. Faux leather pants—faux because you don't smell cow skin—and a black tank top. She makes it to the window. Her arms are tattooed: all blackwork. Horses. Trees. She's rather monochromatic in a beautiful way. Like a pencil drawing you would design for your personal enjoyment. Bronze skin, dark eyes, and hair. You look at your own hand; it's a starscape of freckles.

You look back up to see Mer stepping back from the window quickly. She calls out, "Red!"

That's you. You would have known from her tone, even if you hadn't looked away to reflect on your own colorations. As you step out into the path, you notice a bright glow coming from Mer. You hear and see the glass window crash outward, followed by a dark figure. *And another.* Light washes the alley and you see nothing for a second. You blink to clear your eyes, to adjust. Mer has transformed. She stands as tall as two men. Her lower body has become equine. She has four hooves and white fur. Her toned abs meet her lower body in a vee shape. Her silhouette is imposing, beautiful, and powerful.

Your eyes are drawn to her navel and then you glance up. Her long black hair lies atop each breast, obscuring them, and her eyes glow a startling amber. She pulls a bow and arrow from her back. You can't recall if the weapon was on her back before or not. *And where did her clothes go?*

Before you can think to move, she has downed the first figure with an arrow to the shoulder and is turning away from the second hooded figure. You grin. She's about to kick him to the curb with her massive and powerful hind legs.

You see a third figure skulking just inside the broken window. They are carrying a small bundle of *something*. You advance and realize you move more quickly than you expect. You arrive in front of the hooded form as it steps over the window ledge. Their eyes and their markings catch you off guard. When you imagined cat-people, you assumed lions, maybe panthers. This person is…well…an orange tabby. Their large eyes broadcast their emotions more readily than you assume they'd prefer. Slit pupils become round as saucers. You have to fight the urge to feel sorry for them. That is, until the bundle starts crying.

A human child! The fiends! Kitten poker, but in reverse…

The feline throws the child past you. You dive and roll, moving like lightning, catching the infant and shielding their body with your own. You rise to your feet again quickly. Three long steps and you have the fiend by the hood, revealing their pointed ears, and bringing them to their knees. The *werekitten* stands, turning to face you. You shield the child as the *Morris look-a-like* lifts their hazardous-looking claws.

"Morris my ass. You're more like a *Tabby Kreuger*," you say, stunning your opponent.

They drop their claws. "Been so long since I saw a vamp, I forgot how specist you all are."

You hide your shock. Morris isn't Morris. *She* sounds more like a Morri-sa. *Maybe… Clawrissa.*

Face to face with *Catwoman*, you don't dare look over your shoulder to check on Mer, but you hear her.

As you stare down your prey, you feel a sharp blow to the back of your head. As you spin, a claw grazes your throat. The infant is pulled from your arms from behind you as the beads from your cross necklace fall like rain to the cement below. A black-furred cat-person with green eyes laughs in a masculine voice as he kicks you. Then, he and *Krueger* retreat into the night.

You briefly feel woozy, and the world seems to spin, but you return to level quickly. Something has changed. You feel your body move, but you aren't in control. You strut toward Mer, who is on the ground, in human form, *and clothed*, once more clutching her waist.

You say things you don't want to say. "Hey, horse-girl. Looks like you got more pussy than you could handle, eh?" You are surprised by your accent. It's Irish maybe, or… No, definitely Irish.

Mer looks up at you, eyes angry and disappointed. You can tell that she knows something has changed and that she's in danger.

"Seems you lost as well, Red."

You laugh, though you don't want to. "No, I'm found. *Red* is gone." You want to rush to Mer's side. To tend to her wounds, hold her. You want to go after the cats and their prisoner. But you're just a passenger in a runaway vampire.

"What?" Mer's jaw hangs in astonishment. "Who are you?"

You feel your body curtsy. "Cordelia Connor. It's a pleasure to finally meet you."

Mer, with great effort, forces herself to stand. She limps past you and kneels to gather the beads from your necklace. You feel Cordelia smile. You want to wipe her grin off your face, violently. You can feel what she wants to do to Mer. To your friend. To this woman you have feelings for.

Cordelia extends your hand. "Get up, love, they're only beads."

Mer nods and takes the offered hand.

You feel dizzy.

* * *

You find yourself staring into the eyes of a beautiful woman. She's tall, athletic, and has the most amazing hair. "Hi," you say.

She wipes tears from her eyes with the hand you aren't holding and grins. "Hey you."

You blush. "It kind of looks like we were about to kiss."

She laughs. "Maybe we were."

You feel a cold object between your hand and hers.

She notices your downward glance. "That cross is from your necklace. I think we broke it making out."

"You saved it for me?"

"I did." She touches your face. "You won't remember this. You have trouble making new memories. I'm Meredith, and you and I are best friends."

You laugh. "Can we be more?"

She pulls you close. "Yes. I want that. But I need your help first."

* * *

Three weeks later.

You wake in a dark room. Your head feels heavy. You sit up and feel a pang of guilt, but then you remember something that gives you hope. A woman named Meredith and a child the two of you rescued. You call out, "Mer?"

The bedroom door swings open. "Thank Dionysus you're awake!"

You shield your eyes from the light streaming in from the open door. Mer quickly closes it and sits by you on the bed. She takes your hand. "How do you feel?"

You smile. "I feel like it worked. I'm so happy to see you."

Mer nods. "What do you remember?"

You sigh. "More than I want to."

Mer takes a deep breath, but you squeeze her hand before she can speak. "But…I want to start with the important things."

Mer nods silently.

You caress the back of her hand with your thumb. "I remember waking up with no memories at least a thousand times. The last 400 or so times, *you* were the first thing I saw. You've been there for me even though I didn't even remember who you were."

"You couldn't."

"Nevertheless, you were there. Every time since that first time. I'm a lucky girl."

"How so?"

"Falling in love, at first sight, is supposed to be rare. I did it hundreds of times in two years. And you stood by me even though my memory broke your heart over and over."

"Worth the wait. Once I knew the necklace was the linchpin of your curse, I knew I could find a witch which could fix you," Mer says, laughing at her terrible pun.

You grin as she kisses your hand. After a brief moment staring into her eyes, you continue. "But I also remember 211 years living as Cordelia Connor." You use your former accent on the name sarcastically.

"She's gone," Mer says. "Unless…you want her back."

"No! Never. But…"

"What?" Mer's eyes are wide as saucers.

"I have a lot of good to do to make up for Cordelia's crimes. I was… horrible."

Mer catches a tear with a soft kiss on your cheek. "But I know you, Red. You're a beautiful soul. And I think there's a baby girl at child protective services that is a very big check on the good column."

You nod and take a deep breath. "I'm going to have to ask you for more help. I'll understand if you say no."

Mer lets go of your hand to touch your face. "You don't have to ask. I am yours, and you are mine."

You nod and take her wrist. She also takes yours. "I am yours, and you are mine," you repeat, not fearing the consequences. The pop culture reference is in your memory again. Cordelia was an avid fan. Congrats, you just got married!

After a full minute of silent smiles, you stand in front of Mer. You speak excitedly, and with your hands. "I say we build a team. We save the neighborhood, maybe even save the whole city! I won't stop until the nights are safe."

Mer nods. "I'm in."

"Partners?"

"Yes, partners." Mer stands in front of you. You know she will stand beside you no matter what. She already proved that. You kiss the love of your life, finally hopeful that you might not have to forget her ever again.

ABOUT THE AUTHOR

A.C. Merkel is the Author/Creator of Her Name Is Murder series and Witch VS. Witch.

Merkel creates characters you'll love by infusing stories with empathy, magic, wonder, music and inclusivity.

A.C. is a founding member of https://Queerindie.com

There's Romance Afoot

NT Anderson

Bursts of early morning sunlight filtered through the trees, momentarily blinding Marisa as she weaved her truck down the mountain road. It didn't matter if she had to squint for a few seconds; she knew the twists and turns of this trail like the back of her hand.

Turning onto the main road, she continued her descent toward the town at the base of the mountain. She reached the mist exactly where she was expecting it and backed off the gas a little, knowing that before long, her vehicle would be enveloped by thick fog. At home, in her isolated cabin in the woods, she was above it as the mountaintop peaked out over the pea soup in the valley. This time of year, in town, it would always be a different story when long autumn nights cooled the ground to the dew point.

Marisa drove past the large, historical homes that lined the road into town, peering through the gloom to see outdoor lights that had been left on through the night. She could just make out the pumpkins, fake cobwebs, and skeletons that adorned the various porches in preparation for Halloween.

Her zip code wasn't known for hauntings by various spooks and ghouls, a fact for which she was eternally grateful. The old town, formed in 1803, could have been a prime target for souls trapped in the *in between*, but no such stories circulated among the longtime residents. Indeed, the town was in danger of being boring in that respect, which suited Marisa just fine. She didn't have time to lose sleep over the supernatural, a concept she believed in but wanted no part of. Especially when she was tucked into bed at night all by her lonesome in her woodland cabin.

It was too early on a Saturday for the town to be bustling yet, so Marisa had no trouble finding a parking spot close to the door at Walmart. As she gathered her purse from the passenger seat, she looked over to see a man pulling in right next to her. His uncommon muted auburn hair made her do a double take.

Red head. Like me, she noticed.

As her eyes scanned him, she made a couple of quick observations. First, she noted he didn't look at all familiar. Second, he was also *very* handsome.

They both stepped out of their trucks in unison and headed toward the store. Marisa, who was parked a little closer, by rights should have been a few steps ahead, but the stranger was easily six-foot-four, and his long strides quickly overtook hers. As he passed her, she glanced in his direction, flashing him a friendly smile. The man caught it and hesitated a moment while giving her a smoldering stare before hurrying faster into the store.

Definitely handsome, she thought. *But also a little odd.*

After perusing the dairy aisle, Marisa found herself standing three feet back from an intimidating wall of cereal boxes, trying to make her choice for the week. Halfway down the aisle, the enigmatic stranger from the parking lot was doing the same exact thing. He was the rugged kind of man for whom she had a soft spot. Kind of reminded her of a lumberjack.

Other than the muzak piping through the store's ceiling speakers, it was eerily quiet. Marisa decided to take a chance and subtly shuffled sideways until she was within a comfortable conversation distance.

He bent his head forward and rubbed the back of his neck.

"Got a kink?" Marisa asked.

The stranger turned to face her. "Not really. Just always stiff," he replied. "Especially in the morning."

His voice was deep and gritty. It flowed into her ears and through her body like a comforting song.

"I work at the salon over on Merman Street, and we have a really good masseuse. She could probably help with that."

"Oh? And what do you do there?"

Marisa turned to face him. There it was again—that same heated look he'd given her in the parking lot. It sent a shiver up her spine. "I'm, uh…a stylist." It wasn't often that she felt tongue-tied, but she did her best to recover. "Cut and wash hair, mostly."

"I think I'd rather have my hair washed than get a massage." The man turned back to the cereal selection.

"Really? Most people would disagree," Marisa remarked.

"Guess I'm just…different." He shrugged. "But there's too much hair to wash. It would be a chore."

Marisa eyed the shaggy mop on his head. It looked like organized chaos, and she wanted to reach out to run her hands through it. "That would hardly be a chore," she said.

He ran his fingers across the top of his head. "Oh, this." The man thought for a moment. "Well, you're not seeing it at its worst."

We're leaning toward odd again. But there's still something about him…

He took a box of Fruity O's from the shelf. Marisa chuckled.

"What?" he asked.

"Nothing. Sorry." She gave him a quick once-over. The man was built like a linebacker. Tall, broad chest, big hands, and it didn't look like he had an ounce of fat on him. "Just expected you to choose something more… adult."

He stared at her.

"You know…healthier." Marisa stood on tiptoe, trying to reach a box of granola on the top shelf. The man moved closer and took it down.

"I'm not into tree bark." He smiled as he handed it to her.

"I wish I could eat Fruity O's, but I spend enough time at the gym as it is."

"Where do you work out?"

"Over at Griffin Fitness on Chimera Road. You?"

"I…run. I'm a runner."

"Oh, cool."

"And a hiker. Lots of hiking."

"You've come to the right place for it," Marisa said. "Are you new around here? Or just passing through? I haven't seen you before. I'm Marisa, by the way."

"Yeah, I'm new." The man paused, his eyes nervously scanning the store-brand cereal section before finally introducing himself. "I'm…Sam."

Marisa smiled, hoping she was keeping a neutral expression on her face while her insides melted. At thirty-two years old and a lifelong resident of a town with a *very* limited dating pool, she'd already gone out with the handful of guys who interested her. Now she felt resigned to the single life, living out her days with only her hound dog Tucker by her side.

"Well, it's nice to meet you, Sam." Marisa hesitated, trying to decide if she could take this impromptu meeting another step further.

Am I seriously picking up a guy in the grocery store?

"Have you found everything you need?" she asked awkwardly.

Sam looked from Marisa to the Fruity O's box sitting in his basket.

"Around town, I mean. Do you know where everything is? Or can I help with anything?"

Sam shuffled his feet and looked at the floor. "I'm good. Kind of a loner. Keep to myself a lot, so I don't plan to come into town too often."

"Where are you staying?"

"Up the mountain. Near Lake Believe."

Marisa tilted her head in question. She lived a little farther up the trail from Lake Believe, and she knew the handful of people who had homes there. "Oh, really? That's not far from me. Did someone move?"

Sam looked startled. "Oh. No. I'm…camping."

She thought a moment, then remembered there were a few campsites along the eastern bank of the lake. As far as she knew, nobody had used them in years. "I thought those sites were abandoned."

"Well, like I said, keeping to myself."

"Just be careful out there. Lots of troublesome critters in these woods at night."

"Troublesome?" Sam frowned.

"Yeah. We have the pesky ones, like racoons and deer, but also lots of bears and, sometimes, coyotes."

Sam's frown turned into a smile. "I'll protect my Fruity O's at all cost."

"Sounds like you're set then." Marisa smiled while feeling a little sad inside that their conversation seemed to be coming to an end. "I'm just up the mountain from you…" *Am I seriously going to tell this guy where I live?* "…on Legend Lane." *Yup.* "You know, if you need anything."

"Thanks. I appreciate that." Sam turned his cart to exit the aisle. "See you around."

"Yeah. See ya."

Marisa watched him walk away. She was still looking in his direction when he turned around and gave her what she interpreted as a sad smile.

Why is he just leaving without asking me out, or at least getting my number, if he's interested, too?

All manner of possibilities began to drift through her mind, including thoughts that maybe he had a wife somewhere or was on the run. And no one runs from good things.

Couldn't think of that before you told him where you live?

After giving herself a mental facepalm, Marisa remembered she had self-defense capabilities that should concern anyone who thought of messing with her. Between that and Tucker, she didn't worry about much and felt pretty capable of taking care of herself. Even if he was a serial killer.

Oh, stop it, Marisa, she scolded herself. *I'm sure the only cereal he's killing is that box of Fruity O's.*

With her shopping finished and paid for, Marisa made her way out to the parking lot where she found Sam loading his groceries into the back of his truck. The fog was lifting, and the parking lot was busier now. Her sleepy little town was slowly coming to life.

Marisa lowered the tailgate of her truck and glanced sideways to see Sam smiling at her. He opened his mouth as if he wanted to say something, then closed it before walking over to help her load her bags.

"What's up?" she asked as Sam placed the last two bags into the bed and closed the gate.

Leaning against the truck, he looked down at her. He was so tall that she had to tilt her head back to see his face. His smile was warm, his eyes were kind, and…what was that scent? Fresh, like the forest after a rainfall.

"I'm sorry, Marisa."

His voice snapped her back into the moment. "For what?"

"I think…I think we had a connection in there. And I'd really love to ask if we could get together again. Somewhere outside of the cereal aisle."

Here it comes, thought Marisa, her heart suddenly thumping faster in her chest.

"But I just think it's best if I keep to myself. I'm not really…dating material."

Marisa hoped the look on her face didn't register how surprised—and disappointed—she was to hear his statement. Clearly, she hadn't been doing a good job of keeping her interest in this stranger a secret.

"I don't know what the definition of 'dating material' is, but I'm pretty sure that two single people and some good chemistry is all that's needed to get started. You *are* single, aren't you?"

Sam nodded. "I'm single. I'm just very much…misunderstood."

"Oh, well…" Before she could form a rebuttal, a large black bus followed by a tractor trailer caught her eye as they pulled into the parking lot. This wouldn't have normally been anything out of the ordinary, but the lettering on the side of the bus gripped Marisa's attention.

"I'll be damned," Marisa muttered, nervously wringing her hands.

Sam turned to see what had distracted her. "Are you fucking kidding me?" he whispered.

The bus came to a stop at the end of the row where Sam and Marisa stood. Within seconds, everyone in the lot, except for the two of them, was hurrying to surround it.

As the commotion progressed, Sam turned to Marisa. "I have to go. I really am sorry."

Marisa stood speechless, her eyes shifting between the ruckus around the bus and Sam's abrupt departure. She stepped back to give him room to maneuver his truck out of the spot and watched as he drove away. All Marisa could hope for was that she'd run into him again, and maybe he would change his mind. A simple dinner to get to know each other a little better seemed harmless enough.

Her attention turned back to the bus and the people surrounding it who were now loudly proclaiming statements like "I saw it near my barn last week!" and "Come to my house, and I'll show you!"

All she could do was shake her head and hope for the best as she got into her truck and drove past the black bus with the large white, fancy lettering that said:

Searching for Sasquatch
America's #1 investigative series

* * *

Later that night, half the town, Marisa included, crammed themselves into the high school gymnasium to hear what the *Searching for Sasquatch* people had to say. The question on everyone's mind was, *Why are they here?*

The question on Marisa's mind was, *When will they leave?*

By the time she arrived, it was standing room only, so she leaned against a wall at the back and listened to the conversations going on around her.

To her left:

"I swear, I saw one of those things on my way to work a couple of years back. It was running through a field heading for the mountain. Smaller than I thought it would be."

"You're so full of shit, Bob. Does Santa Claus leave you nice presents every Christmas, too?"

To her right:

"Jake was all in a tizzy last week. He swears he saw it take one of our pumpkins off the back porch."

"Oh, I know! I've heard they're absolute thieves! Steal anything that isn't nailed down."

Marisa closed her eyes and asked herself what she was doing in this crowd. Of course, she knew all about the obsession some folks had with the creature known as Bigfoot, but she herself didn't see the fascination. As a matter of fact, she wished the hype would die down.

She'd seen all the documentaries, read all the books, and knew that the common concept of Bigfoot was a tall hairy monster that stomped around forests, occasionally being caught on camera. She'd lived at the top of the mountain by herself long enough to know that many different sights and sounds were represented in the woods. Particularly at night.

Could such a thing exist? Absolutely. Especially if it was smart enough to either blend in or avoid town altogether. The bold-faced theft of Mr. and Mrs. Klops' pumpkins notwithstanding.

The gymnasium lights dimmed slightly, and a man walked out to a microphone that was set up in front of a long table where eight chairs sat vacant. Marisa recognized him as Mr. Ness from the town council.

He held his arms up. "Everyone quiet down, please. We're about to get started."

Raucous conversations turned to hushed murmurs before the audience went silent.

"Thanks. Okay, so, as you all know, our town will be hosting the award-winning television series *Searching for Sasquatch*."

Loud applause filled the room.

"I know, I know. This is really exciting, folks." Mr. Ness beamed a huge smile at the crowd. "So, the ladies and gentlemen from the show wanted to have this townhall-type of meeting before they get started. They're going to let us know how they operate, where they'd like to conduct their search, and what they need from us. So, without further ado, I give you the esteemed investigators and producers of *Searching for Sasquatch*!"

Marisa smirked as Mr. Ness declared the name of the show in a "Let's get ready to ruuuumble" voice.

Six men and two women filed out from the side of the gym and took their seats. One of the men near the middle of the group pulled his microphone forward, introduced himself as Jon, and began presenting the rest of the group.

Two men and both women made up the investigative team. The other four men had behind-the-scenes roles on the show.

Apparently, they'd had several letters and emails from townsfolk who wrote to tell them Bigfoot had made a home in the area. A couple of the emails included photos and video, too. This recent uptick in activity, along with a few sporadic reports over the last couple of decades, was enough to convince them this was a town worth investigating.

After all of that was explained, they asked for input from the audience. Marisa saw about twenty hands shoot into the air, and one of the producers pointed to a man in the third row, who Marisa recognized as Mr. Champlain, or Champy as most of the town's residents called him.

Champy stood to address the panel. "I was sittin' in my van the other night out by the scenic overlook, and I saw one of them things come running out of the woods. Stopped dead in its tracks when it saw me, then turned around and hauled ass back into the tree line."

"Told you all that ganj you smoke would get to you sooner or later,

Champy," someone in the back declared.

The crowd broke out in laughter. Marisa stifled a giggle.

"What is this shit?" a woman from the middle of the room asked.

She stood up, and Marisa saw it was Sarah, a former co-worker from the salon before Sarah fell ill and had to take an extended leave of absence.

"I thought this was a town meeting to air grievances. My field of give-a-fucks is barren for this nonsense unless someone can do something about all of the park benches being in a sad state of disrepair."

The Bigfoot panel exchanged awkward glances with each other before Jon spoke again. "As a matter of fact, ma'am, one of the missions of the show is to help out the local communities we visit, so if replacing park benches is a concern of yours, we'll take it into consideration."

Sarah looked surprised. "Oh, well, that's different. Okay, then. Put me in front of a camera, and I'll swear I saw a hundred of those Squatch things running right down Main Street. I'll even say I had one in the salon once for a haircut."

Jon chuckled. "Our thanks to you, but that's not how this works. We don't want to air any untruths."

"Suit yourself," Sarah said before she walked out of the gym.

That's just great. In a matter of seconds, they've managed to endear themselves to the town and earn everyone's trust by being so honest. Marisa ran her hand through her hair as her concern grew.

"Can I finish my story now?" Champy piped up.

"How'd you see Bigfoot through all that smokey haze in your van, Champy?" someone yelled across the room.

Two more voices chimed in…

"Wait…"

"It's true."

Marisa scanned the room and saw two brothers, Barry and Andy, walking over to where Champy stood. They turned to face the panel.

"We hang out at the overlook, and we've seen it, too," Barry said.

"That's because y'all are Champy's dealers!" a heckler announced.

"Bill and Ted's Excellent Adventure!" another one called.

"No, really!" Andy spoke up. "We think it's a shapeshifter of some kind."

The crowd laughed, but Jon held up his hands for quiet. "Go on, son. We've heard this theory before, but tell us what you know."

"Well," Andy continued after clearing his throat, "Barry and I saw it come out of the woods one night. When it spotted us, it turned and ran. But like five minutes later, this tall dude comes walking out of the woods. We said, 'Hey, man,' and asked him what he was doing out there so late at night. He said he'd been *hiking*, man. But, I mean, who goes hiking at night, right? So, we asked him if he saw the Bigfoot, and he got real freakin' nervous looking and said no. Then he just went back into the woods. Man, I swear, we weren't even smoking that night."

"Not the strong stuff, anyway," Barry muttered.

The large room filled with murmurs. Marisa saw some people nodding their belief while others shook their heads.

After a minute, Jon whistled to get everyone to settle down, then went on to explain what they needed. More photos, more videos, descriptive encounters, and exact locations. Some of their crew would be handing out forms to anyone who wanted one, and they'd be in touch in a couple of days to begin interviews.

On her way out, Marisa waved away the form for those who wanted to share their Bigfoot experience but took a flyer detailing how the show would be filming at night and what anyone who lived near the woods should expect. She thought about Sam and the likelihood that the show would be causing a ruckus near Lake Believe.

Marisa searched the crowd on her way through the school parking lot with no expectation of seeing Sam, so she was more than a little surprised to spot him hurrying toward his truck across the road.

She jogged in his direction and called out to him when she was nearly caught up. "Sam!"

He continued toward his vehicle without acknowledging her.

"Sam!" Marisa called again when she was just steps behind him.

Sam turned suddenly, causing Marisa to run smack dab into his chest. He caught her in his long arms. When she recovered herself and stepped back, she saw the alarmed look on his face.

"Sam, what's wrong? I didn't expect to see you here. Were you in the gym the whole time?"

"I was outside the doors in the hall. Marisa, I...I have to go."

"Why? What's going on? You look like you've seen a ghost."

"It's just...not a good idea for me to be around here right now."

Oh, for heaven's sake, he is a criminal!

"I haven't done anything wrong," Sam continued, as if reading her mind. "So please don't think badly of me."

Marisa turned toward the parking lot where many people still milled about, discussing the excitement of the national attention they'd soon be getting. "I guess that's a lot to deal with for a self-proclaimed loner."

It's a lot to deal with for me, and I've lived here all my life.

She turned back to Sam, who was staring at her with longing in his eyes.

"You were right," he said. "About the chemistry. And I think we have it. But I'm sorry…it's not safe for me here right now. And I never will be dating material."

"If you haven't done anything wrong—"

"Marisa!" a woman called.

Marisa spun on her heel to see the owner of the salon, Jax, waving and walking in her direction.

"I have to go," Sam said. He leaned over and kissed Marisa.

It was brief but soft and sweet and everything she could have asked for in a first kiss. Then he was in his truck, and she was watching fading taillights before she could even register what happened.

"Ooo, who was that?" Jax asked as she got closer to Marisa.

"I don't know."

"You don't know? Some stranger just kissed you?"

"No. It's a long story," Marisa answered, turning away from the faded truck lights to face Jax. "What's up?"

"What do you think about all this? I think we should grab a bottle of wine and go into the woods to find this fucker. We can wear the fairy tutus I made last year for Halloween and try to summon shit."

"Jax, what the hell?" But Marisa knew exactly what was going through her boss's head. Jax was always getting into shenanigans with seances and anything otherworldly.

"What? It'll be fun. We can help it escape! If these crazies find it, God only knows what they'll do to it."

Before Marisa could answer, the crowd in the parking lot formed a circle around a truck. Someone stood on the bed, seemingly getting everyone riled up. Jax and Marisa crossed the road so they could hear.

"…and when we find it, we'll run it off the mountain. If we don't do something, it'll steal all of our pumpkins! Jake Klops is already missing some, and I guaran-damn-tee ya it's coming for yours next!"

"I'm worried about my chickens!" came a shout.

"What about my rabbits?" asked a concerned citizen.

Any chance for more people to voice their fears of the unknown was stifled when Jon exited the school, megaphone in hand. "I understand the worries you have," he said, climbing up onto the truck next to the instigator. "We need you to know this is perfectly natural. And since we have no power to stop you from searching for the Sasquatch, all we can do is offer our expertise if you insist on doing so."

The crowd roared with full-fledged mob mentality. Planning began, and from what Marisa overheard, they would be heading out that very night to hunt for the oddity that had supposedly taken up residence in their woods. The terrorizing pumpkin thief. Mr. Gablin, the owner of the town's only hardware store, seemed particularly vocal, no doubt looking forward to the increase in pitchfork sales he was about to get.

Marisa was disgusted. "I'm going home," she told Jax.

"But we could—"

"Be careful if you go out there with this bunch. I've never seen everyone so fired up." Without waiting for a response, she walked to her truck.

* * *

When Marisa got home, she was greeted by Tucker who needed to go out. She flipped the switch for the floodlights that lit up the backyard as she and her dog walked outside together. In the distance, she heard loud shouts that indicated the townspeople were beginning their hunt. Marisa shook her head. If there was something unusual in these woods, she felt sorry for it.

Tucker stopped at the edge of the yard and barked, then ran to Marisa's side where he assumed defensive mode.

"I know. They're all crazy," she said, leaning over to scratch him behind the ears. That's when she heard the crunching leaves.

Marisa stood upright. She reminded herself that it was probably a deer. Worst-case scenario, a bear. After scanning the tree line for just a few seconds, she discovered she was wrong.

Despite its best efforts, the tree it was trying to hide behind didn't fully conceal its large, tall body. It was covered in shaggy auburn hair from head to toe.

Is that a bear? Marisa squinted. Recognition dawned. *No. No way.*

It shuffled on its feet, almost nervously.

Tucker didn't bark. Instead, he sat down, tilted his head, and watched with curiosity.

Marisa backed toward the house, keeping her eyes on it. She didn't want to turn away from it, but at the same time, she felt no real threat.

She reached the door, turned the knob, and stepped inside. Just as she was closing it, the creature leaned its head down and rubbed the back of its neck with a giant hand.

* * *

An hour later, Marisa sat in her living room with a glass of wine. The television was off, and she played no music. The townsfolk posse was making their way up the mountain. Even with her doors and windows firmly closed, they were close enough for her to hear muffled voices.

Her doorbell rang, startling her. She hoped it wasn't one of the rabid searchers in need of something.

Marisa turned on the front porch light first, then opened the door.

"Sam!" she practically shouted with excitement. "This is unexpected."

"Yeah. Sorry. I just…" He shuffled his feet. "You know, there's a lot going on, and I thought I'd…"

"Oh, yeah. I'm sure it's chaos around the lake right now."

Sam nodded, seemingly at a loss for words. Nervously looking around, he locked in on Marisa's small autumn porch display that consisted of a pumpkin and a few gourds. "That's a really nice pumpkin," he awkwardly commented.

"Thanks. Courtesy of Mr. Klops." She smiled wickedly when Sam's head snapped up to look at her.

"But…"

"It started out as a joke years ago when I was a mischievous kid, but I still do it now as a matter of tradition." She laughed. "That doesn't make you think badly of me, does it?"

Sam shook his head. "No. Just a harmless prank. There are lots of things in this world that are harmless and don't deserve judgment."

"I couldn't agree more."

"Hey…didn't Mr. Klops say he saw a Bigfoot take his pumpkin?"

Marisa smiled. "He did, yes."

Sam looked confused. "Was he just making that up? Trying to get attention?"

Shaking her head, Marisa kept smiling.

The grin on Sam's face ran from ear to ear. "We need to talk," he said as he leaned his head forward. She reached her hand out to gently rub the back of his neck.

A gunshot rang out in the distance.

"Better come inside," Marisa said. "It isn't safe out there with all those *humans*."

*N*T Anderson is a published author of steamy romance and the co-founder of the publishing imprint Tepris Press. A lifelong lover of the written word, she spent years working in hospitality, restaurant management, and even pole dancing before becoming a full-time writer in 2009. Nikki's first trilogy, The Acts Series, was released in 2021/2022. More books will be forthcoming in 2023.

In addition to writing, Nikki is also a radio presenter with a catalog of shows for the UK-based audio production company One Flower Two Turtles.

She currently lives in the Endless Mountain region of Pennsylvania When she isn't writing, she can be found sipping rum by candlelight and spending time with her pets — two spoiled dogs and an unruly cat.

Harmony of fire: The Rise of the Sleeping Giants

SJ Covey

George Orwell's novel, The road to Wigan pier, declares Sheffield is built on seven hills. He compares her to Rome. I've never understood this, but everyone I meet tells me. Proud to share the knowledge I already know. I'm Charlotte, Lottie, to my friends. Rome, you can keep your colosseum because I love my city. A child exploring the steep cobbled alleys with moss clinging to their walls, a blanket of nature's making—is where my love affair starts.

Old steel foundries are a stark industrial contrast to the beauty of the rolling countryside of the peaks surrounding her. The city that gives the young me so many wandering adventures. I know her better than my childhood best friend.

Graduating in 2026, I choose my career, wanting to give back, and a law enforcement profession is my choice. My career progresses at warp speed, a natural with a sense of sniffing out the truth. Although I have many opportunities to climb the ranks and take on a division of my own, I shy away from leaving the streets I love.

Chasing a perp up Jenkin hill, one of these seven hills and acknowledged as the steepest hill in the UK. I rue my romanticised view of my home and wish for the flatness of Amsterdam. Breath burns my lungs, sucking in ragged lungful after ragged lungful, urging my legs to keep going.

Don't quit on me now.

Rumbling stops the perp, and I slam on my brakes too.

"What the…" He swings around, all angry eyes and greasy hair flopping into his eyes, accusing me of causing the ground beneath us to shake.

I shrug. "Nowt to do with me. Oh, and you're nicked."

"You'll never catch me, copper." He taunts me.

His first step to run away never hits the pockmarked concrete, cracked and potholed after many years of hard frosts and minimum upkeep from the council. A hairline crack stretches before us. We both stare at the road. Another rumble widens the aperture to a stickman drawing of a hangman game.

The ground beneath us shakes, the crack widens, and the stickman is pulled limb from limb in a sickening twist; he is hung, drawn and quartered, well, perhaps not drawn. A gaping wound in the road is still growing. Perp's foot sinks between either side of the widening hole.

"Argh." He loses his balance. I leap across the widening gap. We stretch, and our hands clasp.

The ground shudders, and in the distance, I hear screams over the din of car alarms of the vehicles lining the street bumper to bumper.

My perps leg still dangles in the abyss between the road's ragged edges. They stretch towards each other to reunite, beginning to contract.

"No." His face contorts in horror at what is about to happen.

The prospect of the tarmac closing around his leg was probably not something he anticipated when beginning his crime spree this afternoon. A sickening crack assaults my ears; I wince, my shoulders drawing level with the tops of my ears. Perp's howl of agony makes my eyes water. Powerless to help, the road closes around his leg.

I press my hand to my ear, engaging my communication channel. "Control, I need a crew with erm jackhammers to dig up Jenkin. Yeah, and erm, we need to close Jenkin. Stat. The road's caught me perp."

"Come again, Lottie. I mean Guv." The voice crackles into my earpiece.

"Yeah, you heard me. Do it, or this guy is going to lose his leg." Double tapping my ear to end the transmission.

"You'll be alright, mate. You ain't losing your leg." My hand grips the man's hand.

"Yer promise?" His eyes swim with tears of pain, his mouth screws up in a twisted expression.

"Yeah, buddy, you're gonna be fine." Patting his hand with my free hand. The colour of my hand starts to whiten with the pressure he is applying. "I'm the guv, and they'll be here quick."

"Can yer 'ere that?" Perp's eyes are the size of those cute little marsupials whose name escapes me.

"Hear what?" My eyes scan the street for the source of what he wants me to hear.

"Exactly, what's goin' on?" His lips are trembling.

I listen intently. Nothing, the sounds of the city I love are not here. No cars, buses, or trams. No people, just silence. Emptiness. This city is without its soundtrack—no buzz of insects, barking dogs, and crying children. Birds… there are no birds.

I stare up at the ice-blue Autumn mid-afternoon sky. It is empty, even the clouds flee leaving an open blue behind the earlier morning's fog.

Another thunderous sound assaults our ears. The viaduct and Meadowhall shopping centre stand silent at the bottom of the hill. Are they frozen? Too far to see people, but why are no cars moving on the M1?

This rumble is deeper than the last.

"Is Sheffield on those plates?" Perp swipes a stream of sweat from his eye. "Saw on the discovery channel 'bout plates or sumfin."

"Tectonic plates? Are you kidding me? We ain't in San Francisco." His ridiculous statement causes me to laugh at him despite his predicament.

The crevice opens a crack. I move fast, clutching under the perp's armpits and dragging him free. He cries out in pain for the rescue mission.

"What was that?" The perp was all eyes. He looks like the Edvard Munch scream painting.

We stare in disbelief. The road is bucking, performing a stiff disjointed Mexican wave.

"Let's shift." Grabbing his forearm, I half carry, half drag him away from the gap in the road, running across a garden. An angry-looking retiree scowls at us for trampling her daffodils.

"Sorry."

A roar fills the sky. Windows shatter, the terrace houses cling to each other for comfort, their inhabitants hiding behind the sturdy walls, which are not feeling quite so sturdy. I see one woman pull the curtains tight in a ridiculous attempt to block out the world.

"This is dispatch," the voice squawks in Lottie's ear.

Touching my ear, "Receiving."

A look flitters across the perp's eye for the briefest of moments. I've seen this look many times before, he's assessing the situation and whether I'm distracted enough for him to hobble away.

My eyes narrow, willing him to dare.

His shoulders slump.

"We're getting reports across the city of earthquakes."

Everyone's jumping on my perps assessment of what's happening.

"Where?" A no-nonsense reply shows I want the details and no idle chit-chat.

"That's the weird thing." The radio cracks.

"What?" Tapping my foot with the hope, he will get to the point before I draw my pension.

"Walkley, Netheredge, Manor, Firth Park and Wincobank where you are. They are all spread out, but we've not had reports from anywhere else."

"What have they got in common?" I don't realise I'm voicing my thoughts.

"Correction, new reports just in from Wisewood, Stannington and Woodseats," the dispatcher relays.

"Hills." Perp rubs at his broken leg with what looks suspiciously like a piece of bone protruding through his jeans.

I gag." You need a hospital. What do you mean, hills?"

The perp looks down. Colour drains from his face within seconds. He turns his head to the side, vomiting onto the cracked, uneven pavement. The contents of his breakfast soak into the crevices.

"Dispatch. I need an ambulance and some backup." Averting my gaze from both his vomit and wound. Seeing what I need in the garden whose daffodils we ran over.

"Do you mind? I need to treat his leg." Nodding at a thick plant support that looks roughly the right length.

The older woman looks at the perp and goes a similar shade of green.

Nodding rapidly to me, she hobbles to her porch and retreats inside her house.

Removing my t-shirt and leaving my white vest on, I tear the tee into four strips and throw the larger piece to the perp.

"Hold it to the outside of your leg, away from the wound." Ripping the plant support from the soil, the bloom it supports seems to hold its own. But when the wind howls up this street like a banshee running from the hounds of hell, it will bend and snap.

Kneeling before him, grasping the plant stick, I lay it next to where he clutches a scrap of my t-shirt. Before he has time to realise what I'm doing, I tie it on with tight knots to hold the splint in place.

"What the—" perp is pointing behind me, back to the road.

Ignoring him, I concentrate on tightening the last makeshift strap. I tuck a stray piece of my long brown hair, wriggling free of my ponytail in all the excitement, behind my ear—shifting position following his stare.

"Holy…" Never finishing my sentence.

A stream of fire joins steam, or whatever it is, pouring from the crack straight into the air.

"Volcano," the perp howls in pain, forgetting his injury, and pushing himself away from the road.

Activating my comms. "Dispatch, I have fire and smoke coming from under the road. Any other reports?"

"Same, same. The helicopters are video streaming to control. It looks like Sheffield is the gateway to hell." Dispatch sounds a little on edge in the safety of the control room.

"Dramatic much." My eyes roll.

"What did you say about hills?"

I can't believe I'm going along with the volcano theory.

"Those places yer said, they're all killer steep hills." He looks whiter by the second, and I'm pleased to hear the warbling of a siren approaching.

"You're right. Hang on, what the hell is that noise? It sounds like a roar. I heard it before when we were getting away from the road." A police car and an ambulance pull up in front of the carnage, which was once a road.

"I'm leaving him with you. I need to go." Without waiting for them to argue, I take off to find where I abandoned rather than parked my car when I took off after the perp.

Inhaling sharply, I spin back to the new arrivals. "What did you say?"

"N-nothin', I didn't say nothin'. No one did." He steps back involuntarily.

Running back to my car, I stumble. My legs can't carry me fast enough. *What the heck?*

The car doors unlock and open on my approach. I slide in, grabbing the water bottle in the centre console; I drink it in huge gulps. No, I can still hear something; it's singing. I can pick out the words by closing my eyes to focus my senses.

Hear me, oh beautiful fields of green corn and maize.
See me, my sunsets, your skies complete with beauty and haze.
Touch my wings, the winds of the south.
Dare to feel the heat of my mouth.

Drago dragar, draaaagoooo dragaaaaaaaa.
We sail, and we soar.
We live, and we roar.
Our tail and our claw.
Your magic, your lore.

"Guv." My comms come through the car speakers, giving me a heart attack. "You're not going to believe what I am seeing."

You're not going to believe what I'm hearing.

"I just watched a man change into a wolf, just like in a horror film. Then another one ran over. They acknowledged each other with a nod and took off."

"I'm sorry, what? Have you been drinking dispatch?" I press a few buttons to bring up his image on my windscreen. He doesn't appear drunk. His mouth opens and closes a few times.

"What's happened to your hair?"

"This is hardly the time to give me hairstyling tips. I've been through a major incident; gimmie a break." I twist the rearview mirror to see how bad my—"What?"

My hair is scarlet. I don't mean auburn or ginger; I mean scarlet.

It looks incredible, to be honest. But…what is happening?

"No, it's fine. I'll go and check out the other locations." Starting my vehicle, I can try and work out what's happening to me when I figure out what is happening on the streets of my city.

"I didn't say anything. I was going to say do you want me to swap and get you off the streets?

"I know." I click the end of the connection and put my head in my hands. Not just a great new look, I'm also tuning into others' thoughts before they voice them. My head is buzzing with the opinions of the people around me. There are a lot of people going through some sort of transition.

The hills. There must be some connection. It can't be a coincidence.

"Sorry, Guv, I need you to come in. All hell is breaking loose at command." Dispatch interrupted my thoughts. "The front desk is overrun with people, erm claiming they erm aren't people anymore."

"Okay, I'm on my way. There appears to be some mass hysteria. I wonder if some weird gas has been released from the crack in the ground?" I am not looking for him to answer more running thoughts by myself. I steer my car down the hill and circumnavigate the island of Meadowhall shopping centre to reach the command centre.

A steady stream of people is all heading in the same direction. Something is not quite right, but I can't put my finger on it. I follow the road slowly into the parking area and make my way through the throngs of people flocking towards my place of work.

My boss, the division commander, is fighting off a barrage of questions at the front desk.

"Lottie." He waves his hands over his head to get my attention.

I can feel my eyebrows twisting in question, barging my way through. "Come on, make way, let me through. Shift." I part a path to the desk and climb up on top of it.

"Love the new look." My boss prods my leg and points at my hair.

"Everyone be quiet. Let's all calm down." Although my voice doesn't rise above the general volumes of noise, they oblige, and silence descends on the reception. A woman sitting on one of the blue plastic chairs has hair the same shade as mine.

Taking my lead from my hair twin, I single her out. "Can you tell us why you are here and what seems to be the problem?"

A general murmur erupts from the crowd of many people grumbling at once. My glare around the room silences them.

"E-erm, I can see things and hear things," she whispers, twirling a strand of her hair, stretching it over her upper lip like a giant moustache.

"Ohhhhh, she can see and hear." Someone helpfully encourages from the crowd with a voice thick with sarcasm.

"I'm a seer." She stands with newfound confidence, puffing out her chest. "Just like you are." Pointing at me, waving her hands in the direction of my hair.

"I developed my erm skills when the ground started shaking."

"Me too." A small petite woman with flowing blonde hair jumps in, taking over the conversation.

A seer, is that what the song I heard was? Someone else's song?

The petite woman tucks her hair behind her ears, revealing what I can only describe as elfin ears.

"You didn't have ears like this before the shaking?" I gesticulate for her to come closer and inspect her. They are real.

She shoves her phone in my face and her face stares back at me. A smiling photo of her with short hair tucked behind human ears.

"I can do magic," a man with a flowing white beard declares. His eyes are lost in his face; if someone asks me to draw a picture of a wizard, this is the guy I will draw.

Crashing, splintering, and breaking of glass stops him from saying more. An extremely hot, mild-mannered-looking guy. Who looks like a pale, dark-haired Abercrombie model standing to my left. Snarls and fangs extend over his lips.

My eyes feel like they are going to explode from their sockets.

"Freaks," the call from the broken window drifts to my ears.

"Oh great." I hop down from the counter, making my way to the window.

An angry mob is straight from a low-budget version of Frankenstein, where they have run out of pitchforks.

"Sorry, Lottie." The division chief, my boss and my friend, regards me with half-closed eyes of sympathy.

"Sorry for what, exactly?" I fold my arms across my chest.

"I, erm, think we should be protecting the humans." He rightly looks down at his shuffling feet. His eyes flick around the non-humans surrounding him.

"We have always been here. We have always walked amongst you. I have fought alongside you. We have just been awoken." How I know this information, I am still determining. Stealing a glance at my fellow seer, she nods in encouragement.

"Fine, I'll handle this situation myself. But know this: you are a coward, always have been, and always will be." Stomping for the door, I don't realise the others are following me.

The fog begins to blanket the city with the onset of dusk, clinging to the tops of the buildings and wrapping around church spires off in the distance. I see the ground fog crawling from the river, eager to reach and meet its counterpart high in the sky.

I am holding my badge above my head. There must be about fifty of them. The guy closest to me has a Rottweiler straining at its lead.

"Listen, I need you all to turn around and calmly go home. Leave this to us. We will find out what is going on." My voice is loud and carries over the crowd.

"She's one a 'em. Look at 'er 'air. It's too pretty to be human. She's a freak like them." Gobby with the doggy points. I turn and see my fellow freaks providing backup, which I didn't request. I fear this is going to get ugly.

"Come on, let's be sensible." Stretching my arms to the side, with a 'we come in peace' motion.

"Freak." A bottle, an actual bottle, flies at my head.

The wizard stops the bottle mid-flight. He holds it in an energy field, tossing it harmlessly to one side.

Several people scream. The mob participants closest to me step backwards, bumping into those behind them. Some are pushing and shoving starts. A group of weres behind me, I could refer to them as a pack, smell the tension and start to shift involuntarily, making matters one hundred times worse.

The vampires smell blood. Not literally but figuratively, setting their fangs twitching.

"Vampires, look at 'em. Look at their teeth." A bigoted woman in her seventies shouts.

Sure, my new vampire friends mean the humans less harm than the humans mean us at this juncture. I place the flat of my palm towards the woman in a stop gesture. I don't see the left hook coming; however, I brace for the jab to my stomach. Going down to the fog-covered, chewing gum-infested car park like a sack of potatoes. The sound which escapes me is something like, "Ouff."

Before I can get to my knees, the sound of a commotion overwhelms me, and some idiot tramples on my hand.

"Argh!" The pain helps me to my knees, where a kick to the ribs greats me.

A horsey roar breaks through the madness. I look from my foetal protection position with my arms hugging my head to witness a charging unicorn.

The unicorn is not pink and fluffy, with floor-sweeping eyelashes. Foam froths at its pulled-back snarling lips, hooves drag back from the floor and tucking its head down, the unicorn unleashes cantering into the crowd, scattering the humans in all directions.

In the carnage, backing away, I realise whatever this is, it affects animals too.

My fellow seer tries to re-enter the command centre. Her face is a picture of terror, and I'm experiencing flashbacks of my riot training.

A disturbance draws my attention back to the fight. The vampires, weres and…

"Oh, is that a minotaur next to that elf?" I ask no one in particular.

The elf with her flowing blonde hair whipping around her head springs high into the air from a standing start going all Ninja, kicking and punching as many people as possible. A witch with a pointy hat carrying an actual broomstick stands next to the wizard from earlier chanting protection spells.

Sirens explode from the underground car park of command. I sigh with relief at the prospect of my colleagues coming to help, screwing my face up in anger when I see in my mind where they are going.

"No way," Twin hair said, grabbing my hand. "We have to do something, you see, don't you?"

I give her a slow nod and close my mouth, which I didn't realise was open.

A roar or several, the like of which put Jurassic Park, the old movie, to shame, causes the mob to scatter. Not knowing what the origin of this bone-chilling sound is, they don't stick around to find out.

"Lottie." I point to myself, shouting my name.

"Florence Jepson." She points at her chest.

"Did you hear them sing?" Pulling the hand Florence holds towards where my car is. The doors open, and we get in.

"Yes, I think, but I'm not sure." Florence twirls a piece of her hair, doing the moustache thing again.

"That's why we are seers, because we hear them. We are connected; they have released us?" I finish for her.

Nodding, Florence engages the lock on the door. Moments before, one of the few remaining humans, who look more like extras in a zombie movie, throws himself at the car, trying to wrench the door open.

I put my foot down, heading back in the direction I came.

* * *

I park roughly at the bottom of where Jenkin hill used to be, and we climb out of the car. The road is so torn up that old cobblestones lie littered, having been dragged to the surface. We are making our way through the rubble of the road.

There he is—my sleeping giant. "Blue," I breathe.

"You are descendants of her, the first seer, making you seers." Blue's scaled snout comes down to be level with us. He's practically planking.

"But how? What has woken you?" I ask.

Florence and I clutch each other's hands. I reach out a hand; the warm steam from his nostrils reminds me of a steam room. There is also the familiar smell of eucalyptus—his last meal before sleeping for centuries.

"Our life force, the ark, was moved, causing us to bury ourselves and sleep. It must have returned and started a chain reaction." Blue flaps his iridescent gossamer wings, stretching them out, twisting his long neck, and clicking each vertebra.

"The chain reaction woke the other seven dragons of Sheffield and me. Our magic enables you to embrace who you are and come out from the shadows to reclaim what is rightfully ours alongside us."

"But..." I have so many questions. I am a seer, and I can see, as can Florence. Humans will not tolerate a takeover, no matter how un-hostile we try to make this. They will call in the army and capture or kill the dragons.

"We must get you to safety while negotiating a way to co-exist." My fingers stretch to Blue's nostril steam, wafting it towards me. The steam washes over me, comforting and wrapping me in its familiar warm scent, sparking long-forgotten memories. "We've missed you."

His snout nuzzles into my neck like a pet Labrador, but much bigger and much warmer.

"Let's go." I start scaling the dragon. The irony isn't lost that I am using his scales like ladder rungs to climb him.

Florence is right behind me. Once atop, I get a firm grip on his thick neck. Florence wraps her arms around me, making breathing somewhat uncomfortable.

Blue runs along the leftover road rubble and gracefully swoops, diving into the air. His wings were soundless through the fog. We leave the city behind.

* * *

Within ten minutes, Blue engulfs the barriers, shutting off the Woodhead tunnels from the public in a burst of billowing flames. The brightest oranges and reds of Autumnal changing leaves. The metal succumbs to the immense heat with a pitiful squeal, and Blue gently touches down.

"If you sing to them, they will come." Blue paces up and down the vast tunnel, crouching to avoid banging his head on the roof.

There is no need to ask him what he means. I can see myself singing the song of the dragons, the song of my ancestors so many years ago.

"Hear me, oh beautiful fields of green corn and maize." I close my eyes and see a glorious emerald green dragon in Dykes Hall Road, Wisewood, jump from the roof of the medical centre and sail over High Bradfield on her way to us. My face hurt from the broad smile, making my cheeks ache.

"See me, my sunsets, your skies complete with beauty and haze." Florence sings, holding my hands and staring through me to…

We both see a bright scarlet dragon with black lips and matching eyes in our shared minds. Smooth, with no scales on her body, she crawls from the remains of Redmires Road. Fog surrounds her with mystery as she takes to the sky.

"Touch my wings, the winds of the south," we sing together in perfect harmony. Blue closes his eyes. A smile spreads across his wide mouth, huge teeth protrude, and he sighs.

We see a graveyard in Derbyshire Lane in the Woodseats area. It is more built up than the previous sighting. Our site is soundless, but we can tell people are scared. A giant black dragon, more enormous than Blue, is stamping around a graveyard, toppling headstones that stood for hundreds of years. His head tilts to one side, and with grace his size should not be capable of, he glides in our direction.

"Dare to feel the heat of my mouth. Drago dragar, draaaagoooo dragaaaaaaaa."

"No." Florence throws herself to the floor, her hands covering her eyes, unable to block out the inward vision of the slain dragon. Its colour has faded to the stone it has lain petrified in for these many years.

"The humans must have caught her as she woke, dear Barella, such a sweet thing she was. We encase ourselves in stone when we sleep and burrow deep underground for protection." Blue explains. A tear trickles from his eye, finding the path of a river along his scaly snout. A loud splash accompanies it falling to the tunnel's concrete—echoing down and back to us.

Florence is in a heap on the floor. I know I need to save the others.

"We sail, and we soar." Continuing where we left, placing a hand on Florence's shoulder. She puts her hand on top of mine in thanks.

Running towards me in my mind is a grey dragon of medium size, eyes of amethyst with a steely determination. His wings spread out, and he is on his way to us. A crowd of humans left chasing air beneath him.

"We live, and we roar."

A neon-yellow dragon flashes into my mind; he does a pirouette in the cul-de-sac he is stuck in off City Road, taking a wrong turn and getting his tail stuck. His snout sniffs the air once, twice, and he soars straight up into the air.

"Our tail and our claw. Your magic, your lore." Singing the last line, Blue bows his head, and his hot misty breath fills the tunnel. In my mind, I see the view from the top of Stannington. The swish of a bright magenta tail demolishes a whole street of semi-detached houses, converting them to bungalows. The dragon is airborne with three great strides, and I have saved the magic.

"Not bad for a beginner." Blue smiles.

I exit the cave, gathering some sticks and wood. At least there is no need to rub sticks together to start a fire; the dragons can help with this. We wait in the tunnel for the others to arrive, needing to work out what we do from here.

"There must be a way for us to live in harmony." I dump the sticks in a heap away from the sight of the entrance to avoid anyone seeing flames from the winding country road which connects Sheffield to Manchester.

"There never was last time; humans are scared and jealous of our magic." Blue blinks slowly, and the first of the dragons lands outside.

ABOUT THE AUTHOR

SJ Covey lives in Penistone, South Yorkshire with her husband and their dog. She has won a few short story writing competitions across various genres. Her short story @BILIGRATES features in 'The Decagon Key.' SJ's debut novel FamiLIES a new adult fantasy, and part of 'The Order' series is due for release in 2023.

Ghost Duty

Peter James Martin

"My name is Josh Raymond, and I'm dead like you. I'm here to help you adjust to an unlife in Limbo and get you started with Ghost Duty. With us lot, your new found family, we'll make it work!" I said as enthusiastically as I could muster.

"Josh, who are you talking to?" Erica asked as she looked over from the table where she and Ben were deep into their pile of board games.

"I'm prepping for when my protégé gets here!" I snapped at her. "Not every day I get the privilege of helping a poor, unfortunate soul." I stuck out my chest like the proud idiot I was.

"Huh, I thought they had a leaflet to do that job, besides, you weren't chosen, just no one else wanted to do it!" Ben said, before turning his attention back to his real focus. "Let's see now…B15?"

"Miss. C3?" Erica responded, a sly smile showing that she knew what she was doing.

"Goddammit!" Ben cried out, followed by his watch beeping at him.

"Bad Deed Debt increased, taking the lord's name in vain!" it screeched at him.

"Oh, not again!" Ben cried out. Erica couldn't do anything for laughing.

The Bad Deed Debt, the whole reason we were stuck in Limbo. Every dead person with that had to work to get rid of it, unless you were sent straight to the other place, of course.

Realising that he'd also lost the game as well as gained a bit longer here, something we were all resigned to, Ben saw the brighter side:

"Okay, how about 16 out of 31?"

Ben and Erica practically lived on that table. They were playing games there when I first arrived at the door, having been searching for a place to be. They took one look at me and invited me to join them in a game that they both trounced me in. Good times.

"I'm going to go and wait in the hallway," I announced to no-one.

"Josh, don't over-complicate things. The new kid is going to be just as confused as you were. Roll with that," Erica suggested. I nodded like I was agreeing, but I was already set on giving the best first impression that I could. I wanted this new soul to not have to rely on the four-page leaflet that is forced onto you when you enter Limbo. I remembered the title page with its 'Sorry You're Dead' in bright red letters. I remembered the other three pages being vague hints on what Ghost Duty would actually be and what kind of existence I'd expect in Limbo. None of that was newcomer friendly.

A knock at the door caught my attention, and I raced there, almost knocking over Fiona as she came down the stairs.

"You're keen, aren't you?" she said, smiling. "Off to a haunting?"

"Nope, something even better!" I replied, opening the front door to an immense, dazzling light. "My protégé is here!"

"Josh is playing babysitter!" Ben unhelpfully shouted from the other room..

"I'm not a babysitter! I'm just helping the newcomer adjust! Working with them, guiding them, helping them learn the rules!" I explained, trying to keep calm.

"So, a babysitter?" Fiona gave a confused look.

"I'M NOT A BABYSITTER!"

"Which one of you, unlifer's, is the agreed babysitter? I've got forms you need to sign in triplicate," an angelic voice said through the hazy light. I didn't need to look at Fiona to know that she had that carefree smile on her face.

"That would be me?" I said, raising my hand, and a wad of paper was thrown at me, knocking me to the ground with a thud. I may be dead, but the impact hurt. A pearl white pen was thrown at my head.

"That's my last pen, so if I can have that back when you're finished, please?" the angel asked politely, though I don't know how sincere they were since they threw the pen at me. I filled in all the forms as they asked, signing my name at least 16 times. Finished with them all, I hurled the forms, and the pen, back through the doorway to the obscured angel.

"These appear to be in order. Here is your charge, good day," the angel sounded like he was handing over a parcel instead of a soul.

The light dissipated and in the doorway was a guy who looked maybe a year or two younger than me. His wispy blonde hair, blue eyes would have marked him out as one of the popular kids going by my time in school. Now I should point out that I didn't know where this person had come from. It wasn't like Limbo had dedicated parts for each country. To wit, no one I was currently housed with had set foot in England.

"My name is Josh Raymond, and I'm dead like you. I'm here to help you adjust to an unlife in Limbo and get you started with Ghost Duty. With us lot, your new found family, we'll make it work!" I repeated my intro perfectly, hours of practice paying off. My charge blinked a few times, his mouth slightly agape before he even uttered a word. In his hands was that stupid leaflet.

"Urm, hi? I know I'm dead, the others wouldn't shut up about it." he replied. I heard that crack in his voice, like he was on the verge of crying, which was to be expected.

"So!" I said, putting on my best smile. "What's your name? Where are you from?"

I thought I'd put the newcomer at ease, get a nice conversation going.

"My name? My name is Morten Ossum, I'm from Norway." Morten stepped through the doorway and gave the place a once over. "This is Limbo? I don't understand any of this."

"No one does!" Fiona said as she passed us by. "You'll fit in well with that line of thinking!"

"Who's she?" Morten asked, a bit flustered.

"Oh, her? That's Fiona, one of my, I mean, your house mates here! There's four of us in total. Guess five now with you," I answered.

"Five? Who are the other people?"

"Well, there's you, me, Fiona, Erica and Ben. We're all from different countries, and some of us from different times. You get told some great stories. Anyway, now that we've broken the ice, let's talk about what you'll actually be doing here!"

"Broken the ice? What are you talking about? I was in heaven, then an angel told me that this thing called a bad deeds debt was too high to let me in! Then I was brought here. I have no idea what's going on!"

I should point out here that there's a strange time effect between Limbo and Heaven. While poor Morten here was given exactly zero warning of what was about to happen, I was told a week in advance.

"Okay, so the 'bad deeds debt' is something we acquire in life. If it's too high, then we don't get into heaven, hence why we do Ghost Duty, to pay it off, simple right?"

"But I never did anything wrong in life! I did as I was told, when I was told."

"So did I, but you're here, I'm here, we're all here!" I wasn't giving much thought to how I was sounding at this point. I was just working from my script.

I saw the panic start to rise in Morten's eyes, but I'd expected this from someone fresh from the queue at the pearly gates.

"Look! Let's just move on! House tour!" I grabbed Morten's hand and dragged him from the hallway and into the living room.

"Once you get used to this place, you won't think of it as anything other than home!" I lied. "This is the living room where we get to watch the goings on in the mortal world we haunt on this fantastic, 28 inch TV screen!"

Stop laughing, that's all we had.

"We still get news channels in Limbo? Who would put a system in place like that!" Morten asked what would be considered a good question. However, it was one I didn't have an answer to, so I swiftly moved on.

"And this is the kitchen! We've got a four seater table and…that's it." Maybe a tour wasn't the best idea.

"Maybe next time, don't finish the tour in the kitchen," Ben said as he pulled another board game out of the pile. "You two want in on this action?" he motioned to me and Morten, who looked puzzled, thought he finally spoke:

"How can you all be so calm about this?" Morten asked Erica. "We're all dead?"

"Crying about it won't change anything. We're all dead so we might as well have some fun, especially here in Limbo," she said, smiling in return. I had a flashback to when I arrived, when she had said the exact same thing.

"I…" Morten started to say.

"Listen, kid, we've only just met, but I gotta say, best thing to do here? Unwind," Ben added.

"He doesn't need to unwind! Well, not like that. I've got everything under control! I know what it's like. I've been feeling exactly how he is! I'm going to help him like no one helped me!" I protested.

"You mean like how we helped you?" Erica pointed out with a raised eyebrow.

"Oh! I remember that!" Fiona said cheerfully from the back door, where she liked to sit and watch the strange clouds of Limbo go by, "You were so down back then, but we all chipped in to help you!"

"Is there more to this place?" Morten asked, his voice rising from a squeak, interrupting.

"You talking about Limbo, or this house?" Ben asked in return.

"Both?"

"Technically no, I mean for all the angel's care, we rest here. That's why we make our own fun!" Ben put his arm around Morten, pulling him closer as he waved his hand in front of him as he spoke.

"Yeah, you're not going to find anything like arcades or a cinema here. The TV does show movies from time to time," I wanted to add something to this conversation.

"This place wasn't built to be fun, just a dumping place till we have to do ghost duty," Erica looked at her watch, cycling through every time zone imaginable

"You guys keep mentioning Ghost Duty. what is it?" Morten inquired. I cleared my throat, as this was one of the questions I was expecting.

Ghost Duty was the biggest problem I had with the leaflet I had to deal with. You got told the basics, and that was it. I gained my understanding from talking to the others and from those I met on the job. My first haunting, or visitation, as the angels called it, was in England, where I had to haunt a pub with two other lost souls of Limbo. To prove an earlier point about how big Limbo is, I've yet to actually meet them in this town.

"Okay, so you have your bad deed debt. This miraculous number goes down when you do Ghost Duty. What is Ghost Duty though? Simply, we haunt the living. We haunt the ever loving crap out of them. Why? You'll probably ask? Because we have to put the fear in them of the great beyond!" I exclaimed, raising my hands for emphasis.

"Oh? I thought it was to weed out those who did or didn't believe in an afterlife?" Fiona interjected.

"Same, well, I thought it more a test for the true believers?" Ben speculated.

"Know what I think?" Erica said, bringing attention back to her. "I think the angels invented it just to give people in Limbo something to do. It's just a way to keep us all busy."

We all took a moment to ponder Erica's words, even Morten, whose head must have been spinning with all the facts we were unloading on him.

"Nah, there's got to be a plan in there somewhere!" Ben laughed, which started a chain reaction throughout all of us. I did see a smile on the boy's face though. I think he was coming round to the idea that living with us wasn't such a bad idea.

"Maybe we have to keep the idea of ghosts alive so that no one suspects that the afterlife is just you waiting in a line for what seems like forever!" Morten surprised us all with that one. This got a bigger laugh out of everyone.

"I like this kid already!" Ben nudged him with his arm. This scene felt familiar to me as I watched it unfold, except from my memories, I was where Morten was. Seeing him bond with them made me question what good I was doing.

"Come on then kid, tell us all about yourself!" Erica said with good humour. Morten loosened up and started to chat away, leaving me on the outside of the group, and I thought back to when the angels dumped me here.

Since I arrived in Limbo, the first thing I truly learned was that, well, you're alone. The angel dropped me off here, and of course, I knew no one, separated from my former friends, my family. There weren't even any dead relatives to greet me. I got given the accursed leaflet. I ended up leaving the first house I was put in. The residents there cared more about their 'work'. Then of course I found this place, with people who wanted me…

I was going to dwell on this more, but a beeping sound in stereo broke the laughter around me that I wasn't part of. My watch was going off, as was Morten's. Given the time zones back in the world of the living, it meant that we'd most likely have got the same haunting.

I know what you're thinking, what are the chances that me and the new kid would be given the same haunt, on the very first day we'd met? Well, the answer is quite likely, as I'd asked the angels to set it up like that if it was within their power. That last part was a bit of ego boosting. It wasn't a secret that they could do that and more if they really wanted. Despite this melancholy mood I'd found myself in, I resolved to still carry on with my-self proclaimed duty.

"Come on, Morten, we've got work to do!" I said, putting on the best smile I have. "Let's go and scare the crap out of the living!"

While I knew that I could fool Ben and Erica with my smile, Fiona was harder to fool, but I'd grabbed Morten's hand before she could open her mouth and dragged the poor kid to the front door.

"Have fun you two!" Erica's voice trailed off.

"How are we going to get back to earth?" Morten asked. It was probably the question I was waiting for him to ask. While I'd rehearsed my other answers, this one, I knew I'd hit the right way on the first go. I smiled and led the kid to the nearest manhole cover, standing over it like a proud parent.

"Why have we stopped here?" Morten looked around. "Are we getting a bus?"

"There's no cars here, no transport of any sort. Except one." I pointed at the manhole. Morten still didn't look like he was understanding what I was about, which I expected. I knew I would have to give a demonstration.

"See this manhole? Looks just like the ones back in the world of the living, doesn't it? Well, my friend, that is where you're wrong! Watch this, and I mean 'watch' this." If laughing at your own jokes is wrong, I don't want to be right. I pulled my sleeve up and over my watch and held it up over the manhole, which started to creak as it slid open. Sadly, this wasn't a quick process, so you can imagine me standing there holding the pose as the gateway back to the living opened at the speed of a snail who wanted paint to dry slower. I wasn't deterred though, and eventually, the manhole cover was gone, revealing the portal underneath that flashed all the colours of the rainbow in a beautiful display.

"We're going in there?" Morten went to back away, but I grabbed hold of his hand again, and by now, my cheeks were hurting from the smile I was still wearing, but I thought this was better than showing off how I was gritting my teeth in anticipation of the next step, which you guessed it, was jumping in.

"You wanted to know how we were getting back to the world of the living. This is how everyone gets back for Ghost Duty! Are you afraid of heights?" The last part was a thought that popped up in my head, I was meaning to ask it earlier, but you know.

"N-no? Why?"

"No reason!" I hopped in and dragged Morten in with me, my vision being filled with the kaleidoscope of colours that reminded me of a dream sequence in a trippy 60s movie. It's not just your eyes that get a treat, either. There's a sound like a train that always seems closer than it should be, while you get a smorgasbord of smells, none of it good.

You're never in here long, technically speaking, yet it always feels longer while you're in there. This time, it felt like I could probably have watched a full box set of something if I had the means.

Once we were spat out on the other side, my first instinct was to make sure that Morten was okay. Okay, that wasn't my first act. That privilege was given to me trying not to throw up. I was told that I'd get used to it, but I think they were pulling my leg. Oh, and if you want to question how a spirit can throw up, you know about ectoplasm, right? You never questioned where that came from? Anyway, I turned to Morten, who was wide eyed and full of shock.

"W-what was that?" he asked me. My response was to hold my arms out and spin around in the dusk of day. In the distance, there was the hum of traffic, as the living carried on with their lives, not knowing how lucky they were to be alive.

"We're back on earth? I'm alive again!" Morten went to hug the nearest tree, but passed right through it.

"Why did you think you were alive again?" I asked, confused at how he'd taken such a huge leap in logic.

"I-I just thought, being back on earth…"

"We're good old-fashioned ghosts here. Normally we can't be seen, by anyone or anything, but we put the costume on, and that does change… Slightly."

"Slightly? Can't you just give me a straight answer? You're no better than the angels with their stupid leaflet!"

I was positive that he didn't mean that. There was no way I could be worse than that thing.

"What I mean is that we'll be visible to some people and items. Don't you remember being alive and looking at ghost photos or videos on the internet? We're about to make them! Is that being straight enough?" I asked as I floated there. "Oh!" I added, as I had forgotten something that was incredibly important. "We can fly now."

I gestured towards Morten's lower legs, they had been replaced by a wispy trail, the same as my own.

"F-fly!" Morten said in shock, though that quickly changed as the freedom of flight filled him with childlike joy. I believe that everyone felt this when they first gained this ability. There was no one who ever existed that wouldn't have squeed when they threw off the shackles of gravity. Morten was the example of this as he darted around the sky.

"This is incredible!"

I felt smug now. The leaflet had only included the possibility of flying as a footnote, and even then it was more of a warning about crashing into each other.

"We can't fly around here all day though, let's get to the job," I said, as I bade him to follow me. Not that I was going to fly straight there. I mean, I loved flying as well and took the longest route we could to get to where the haunting was. Normally, this place would glow slightly, an effect that only we would be able to see. Today, we were haunting one of my favourite places, Whitby Abbey. I was on home turf, so to speak. As we flew closer, I saw all the lights of Whitby, and with it, a flood of childhood memories that returned as I spotted familiar sights below.

"Are we heading to the glowing thing?" Morten asked, and wiping my tears, I nodded.

"Yeah, just head t-there," I replied, trying to hide the break in my voice. We settled at the top of the 199 steps and took in the view of the town, with the crashing waves giving us a nice ambience..

"This is where we're going to haunt? Looking like this? Won't that be a bit weird?"

I thought for a second about how I was going to answer that. I did have something in mind, but decided against it, and settled on another straight answer, despite how much of a mouthful it was.

"We're going to use an appropriate disguise that will change our appearance to match our location. Think of it as a costume that an actor would wear. This is what I meant earlier about how people will be able to perceive us, take photos and film us!"

"And how do we do that?"

I tapped my watch.

"It's more than just a timepiece, press the button on the left here, and it'll suit you up automatically."

Morten did as instructed, and different clothes appeared to grow out of him, changing his form just like I said it would. Where Morten once floated, there was now a monk, his face hidden within the folds of his hood. I followed suit. The odd feeling of my body's shape being suitably altered was akin to having hiccups. My ghost outfit was the same as his, forming a pair of ghostly monks.

"So…now what?" Morten quizzed. He took his new monk appearance out for a test drive. Noting that his feet still didn't touch the floor, despite the disguise giving us legs back.

"Now we read the support packet and learn the correct method of haunting. We have to keep it consistent with all the other hauntings that people like us have done."

"And this support packet is where?" Morten asked, looking around. I had a feeling he took what I said literally. I held up my watch again.

"It's all on here." I tapped it and the screen changed as reams of letters flew out of it and swirled around us, coalescing into a compactly written report that hovered in front of our eyes.

"So, we're basically going to spend all night going up and down the 199 steps, then at 3 a.m. we're to drift around the abbey and scare the security guards who really ought to be used to this."

I'm not going to lie, since dying, I found Ghost Duty itself to be my element. I don't know if it was because I got to be someone else, or that I was good at it, but something about it spoke to me.

"Can't we pop into people's houses and scare them that way? Who will be coming up the steps at this time of night?"

A solid question, but an easy one to answer.

"For starters, there's a brewery with an on-site bar just behind the abbey. My parents stopped off there once. So there will be people coming down the steps to go home at kicking out time. Unless we've missed that bit, of course. Other than that, you have people who'll come up here to get night time photos, and those who just want the spooky atmosphere!"

Morten looked at me with his mouth agape. Well, I think it was agape; it was hard to see under the hood.

"How did you do that?"

"Do what?"

"Have a complete mood change from when I met you back in the house?" Morten asked.

"I like my job," I said, putting a bit of cheer in my voice. "Now, let's get to work. Those stairs aren't going to climb themselves!"

* * *

It was a weird night, to be sure. To prove me right, there was a group of camera wielding ghostspotters that crept up the steps close to midnight, going by the symbol they all had on their hoodies. I reckoned they were a ghost hunting crew of some description. Me and Morten certainly made their visit worthwhile as we brushed past them, setting off their thermal cameras. The sound they made was music to my ears. While Morten was still a bit sceptical of the whole process, I gave them something to listen to on their little white noise boxes, saying the words 'pray'. It didn't matter how I said the word to them, they heard the voice of an old man, each syllable cracking out of long dead lips. They were over the moon. They snapped plenty of pictures of anything that was in sight, and I think Morten was a vague shadow in one of them, which was par for the course. He eased up into the role towards the end of that encounter, just in time for us to turn the attention to the next part, scaring the guard.

He was a trickier customer than the ghost lovers we'd dealt with on the stairs. I think this was because this was old hat to him. The usual stuff the report suggested didn't have an impact, like making sure he saw us from the corner of his eyes to gently moving items that weren't nailed down. I'd tried whistling and we'd gently upped our game until, in the end, I had to go nuclear. Or to be precise, Morten went nuclear. He went and stood in front of the guard, unloading all his frustrations, about the night, about being dead, really letting the guy have it. Now, the guard couldn't actually hear any of this, nor could he see the kid pretending to be the ghost of a monk who was flipping his lid. I was okay with this as I'd done the exact same thing on my first night as part of Ghost Duty. It was cathartic. Tonight, however, the powers that be made Morten visible at the tippy end of his rant. The guard jumped back half a mile before reaching out, only to grab nothing as Morten was rendered invisible again. I don't think there was a force in existence that would have been able to keep up laughing as we heard the guard's shriek.

A bit unorthodox, but the haunting was complete for another night. I sat with Morten as the sun started to rise, its warm light casting away the dark, and it started the countdown to when we'd be pulled back to Limbo.

"Thanks, Josh," Morten said after a moment's silence.

"Don't mention it!" I said, noting that our monk disguises were fading away.

"Do you think the celebrities do their own hauntings? Like Elvis?"

"Nah, it's us plebs all the way down in various disguises. I know Erica has portrayed a dead famous person, Ben too. My theory is that they're made to haunt as a normal person. Fiona thinks they've just paid to fast track into heaven."

"Do you think we'll learn which one is right?" Morten asked me.

"Who knows, we're all still learning, about everything really. Sorry about today, I had a whole plan in my mind and I think I focused on the wrong things. I should have followed my friend's advice and rolled with it, like you did when we got here," I admitted, changing the conversation.

"You were better than the leaflet."

We both laughed at that, and I was happy that Morten was going to become part of my found family.

Beep Beep!

The beeping was something that I wasn't familiar with and following it, I found the source was Morten's watch, where an image of a halo was flashing on and off.

"What's this mean?" Morten asked, shocked. He looked at me for an answer that I didn't have.

"I've got no idea!" I said earnestly. I had a feeling in my gut but it seemed too fantastic to articulate, till the bloody watch did it for me.

"Bad Deed Debt has been repaid! Bad Deed Debt has been repaid!" An obnoxious, squeaky voice spat out.

"What?" me and Morten said simultaneously. A halo appeared over Morten's head and the overly sweet music of harps played from the watch and my friend began to rise into the sky.

"Josh! Is this really happening?" he asked, but I couldn't bring myself to answer. I was too shocked by what I was seeing.

"I won't forget you!" Morten cried out as he fully ascended, leaving me alone.

"Goddammit!"

My own watch beeped with a very different message on it:

"Bad Deed Debt increased for taking the lord's name in vain," it said with robotic indifference. I seized up, my right eye twitching as everything added up and overwhelmed me, causing me to scream to the heavens, loud enough that even Morten might have heard me.

"THIS ISN'T FAIR!"

Story of my unlife…

The End…but unlife continues!

ABOUT THE AUTHOR

Peter James Martin is Teesside born and bred. He lives for folklore both local and international, often working it into his stories where appropriate. His most well known work is about a long suffering investigator and his talking rat business partner.

Find more musings on his blog at the strange tales of Peter James Martin.

Saviour of the Lost

Samantha Kroese

Magic is visible only to believers. I walk among this bustling crowd without so much as a single look my way. Busy streets packed with people whose noses are buried in the newest electronics, or who are distracted by someone screeching into their ears through headphones or earbuds. All are attempting to drown out the sights and sounds of life around them.

I pause at a store window, not to look at the gaudy wares within, but to study my reflection. I concentrate on my disguise and see only a non-descript woman wearing forgettable clothes. I melt into the crowd around me because they do not believe. So do the others with magic, good or evil, for all who do not believe in them. They walk among us, disguised as I am. Still, when I see them in reflection, I can see the shimmer of their magic like an aura around them. I see the shimmer of wings and a halo on the homeless person across the street who rummages through a garbage can while keeping a careful eye on children playing nearby. The angel senses me and glances up. I meet his gaze and give him a nod of acknowledgement, and he goes back to his duties.

The outline of a dragon towers over a being as it walks past me. I turn to look out of reflex, and a touch of latent fear. In spite of our close proximity, it has not seen me. It is dressed as a businessman and storms through the crowd, which parts before it without being conscious of doing so. Once the danger passes, I decide to lean here against the cold, uncaring stone of the building and watch the crowd through the window.

This is a busy city with many people walking to and fro at all hours every day. I have been here for months hunting my prey with little success, although the experience has not been without its interesting moments. I hear a hiss as someone walks in front of me.

A woman wearing furs clutches the arm of some rich older fellow. The window reflects fangs and red eyes when I gaze into it, but the vampire continues on her way after an almost imperceptible hesitation. I will have to be careful. She has seen the true me and she is hungry. For now, however, she is content to walk away with the human prey so ardently guiding her by the arm.

A sudden giggle that has a sinister undertone reaches my ears. I look down the block to see street children running amuck, weaving through the legs of taller people as though playing a game. My hair stands on end. One of them jumps up onto a post next to me to be certain I have seen them. The reflection I see is a little monster with batlike wings and rows of tiny, sharply pointed fangs. It lashes its long, spaded tail at me before hopping back down to chase the other members of its hunting party through the crowd.

Then I feel her gaze upon me, and I turn and see a young girl, perhaps twelve years old. With her is a male child, younger by perhaps a year or two. Her brother, I conclude. Both stare at me. Time stops and the crowd parts around them. I look all around, searching for parents. I do not see anyone who has missed these children yet.

I pull away from the wall and walk toward them. Once I am within range, the little girl reaches out hesitantly to touch me. The touch burns like fire, an electric shock on a magical level that makes every hidden being nearby stop and take notice. With that touch, I see flashes. Memories of pain and suffering. Unimaginable horrors inflicted on the innocent. Righteous, indignant fury fills me, and my true form reveals itself. With a terrifying scream of rage and a stomp of my magical hooves, the world around me warps, time is unfrozen, the humans flee in terror.

The world once believed that only innocent young women could see my kind. This is not so. I can be seen by any who believe in magic and cling to hope. I grab the children's shirt collars carefully between my teeth and swing them gently upon my broad back and feel their shaking hands bury into my thick mane. I hear the angry roar of the monster who had held them captive as the man, and it is just a man, charges toward me in slow motion. But he cannot reach me, for I exist outside the laws of time and space.

I swing my long neck, a graceful dance of the horn upon my brow to draw magical runes in the air. They glitter and shimmer in rainbow colors before they fade. The magic gives me strength and speed, and I leap as gracefully as a deer over the remains of the shocked crowd. I land on the other side of the street and race past the angel who observes with bowed head. His charges have a chance.

The angel knows that if I have saved them, it is too late for them in this world. They are the lost, the forgotten. They have no angels to guard them and now it is too late. A rainbow bridge appears before us as I race down the street. The monster is still giving chase, and his cries have alerted others. Hungry magical beasts sense the end is near and a feast of youth awaits, if only they can catch it.

No one can catch me. I am made of hope and dreams. Of the last dying prayers of the lost. Of wind and light and magic. Desperate hope clings to my back.

My hooves ring like a soothing lullaby against the rainbow as I touch it, and then we are gliding far faster than any monster could possibly travel. I sense the rush of wind, the taste of freedom, the release of pain and suffering.

We land within a lush, quiet meadow. Brilliant, shining flowers line it, and a crystal blue smooth-as-glass pond shimmers in the center. The figure next to the pond stands slowly, the face filled with compassion and love as the arms open in welcome.

I tell the children it is safe here. No one will ever harm them again. The little boy is the first to follow his instinct and slide from my back. Once he touches the grass, he changes form into a tiny, flawless lamb and bounds eagerly over the meadow and into the arms of the shepherd.

The little girl is older and better remembers the cruelty she and her brother suffered. She clings to my neck, crying relieved tears that he is safe. But she pleads, "Please, beautiful unicorn. Please let me stay with you. It is delightful here, but I do not wish to be a lamb while so many suffer below. Please don't leave me." The other unicorns, resting in the meadow between rescues, raise their heads, alerted by her desperate cries.

I pause. She is too young, I think. I glance at the shepherd who is watching us. I wait for a nod, which finally comes. I turn to look at the girl. "There is only one way you can stay with me, little one. You must become like me. And we must bring others here, which is often dangerous," I tell her gently, trying to dissuade her.

"I want to help them," she insists. Tears dry and are replaced with a grim, determined look.

This does not happen often. It takes a special soul to wish to save others after they have been through so much torment themselves. To rescue others from what they have lived through. Most would prefer to stay here, in the exquisite comfort and safety of the shepherd.

The shepherd walks over, white hooded robe hiding features, for it does not matter what anyone looks like, not here. Yet, the shepherd's approval is clear. A hand reaches out gently to the little girl to and helps her down. As she slides to the grass, she also changes. It is a magnificent transformation and when finished, where once stood a broken innocent, now stands a protector of lost souls.

She prances with joy, shaking her gleaming silver mane, then turns to me. I am to be her teacher. Together we shall hunt and save more lost from the monsters in the darkness. Perhaps one day the living will remember them, and we shall no longer have to leave the meadow of peace.

ABOUT THE AUTHOR

Samantha Kroese is the author of published Dark Fantasy novels including the best-selling Fading Lights Trilogy (Forbidden, Unspoken, Taboo). She has also written the Assassins of Dakaal series (Regret, Ladykiller, and Niyx) and the villain POV novels Restless Dreams of Darkness and The Darkest Sword. She loves to write dark tales about hope surviving against impossible odds and brings a refreshing perspective to the genre. From a young age, her goal has been to write stories that will shine the light of hope for those living in the abyss. She has been writing fiction for nearly thirty years, ran a fantasy writer's critique circle for fifteen years, and has edited works for other authors. She has completed writing dozens of fantasy novels and created thousands of detailed characters. She hopes to be able to present most of them to her reading public in due course.

Samantha is also an avid life-long gamer who enjoys story-driven role-playing video games. A big fan of comic books and superheroes, she enjoys exploring tales of characters who are larger than life and the ordinary people who interact with them. In addition to writing, she is an avid horse lover and an animal rescue advocate, often speaking out for horse rescue and feral cat causes. She writes from the frozen tundra of Minnesota where she lives with her Arabian stallion, that she is convinced is really a unicorn, and her army of delightful rescued cat minions.

The Night Before

Jon Ford

*T*here was safety here.

Relative safety at least.

He wouldn't dare attack her in so public a place.

Too many people.

There's safety in numbers.

It won't last.

The latest news cycles had been dominated by a 'mysterious' global unrest. A world seemingly gone mad, and no one knew why. As usual, the media was rife with unfounded speculation and abstract theory. The more rational-sounding pundits spoke of plagues and pandemics. Others had more outlandish theories; ones the newscasters scoffed about behind their backs.

Monsters.

Supernatural shenanigans.

Yes, they laughed at the concept, but the hard truth was they didn't know what was happening.

But Steffany…she knew.

She knew the *truth*.

But that was all elsewhere in the world. A concern to cities and countries a very long way from the UK. Here, on this tiny island, it was business as usual. Once the crazy, speculative headlines were dealt with, it was on to the customary political tub-thumping, celebrity scandals, and rousing sporting achievements. The public, meanwhile, continued to indulge themselves in re-tail therapy as a distraction. Nobody wanted to think too hard about it. The trouble abroad didn't concern them. Today's news was tomorrow's fish-and-chip wrapper, as they say.

But Steffany *did* think about it.

It concerned her deeply.

She had been quietly sitting here, hugging her knees to her chest, trying to figure out what to do next before it was too late. Her arse was numb. Her eyelids were heavy. Sleep. She needed sleep.

But she couldn't.

She wouldn't.

Tired eyes flitted nervously back and forth, scanning the crowds from under the protective shadow cast by the brim of the baseball cap she'd sto-len. Searching. Trying to spot the face of her pursuer amongst the oblivious. A fruitless exercise. He could be anywhere. He could be *anyone*. She hadn't seen his face. Not clearly. Sometimes she wished she had. Other times, she was grateful she hadn't. Ignorance was bliss, after all.

Sometimes her brain questioned whether he was real.

Did I imagine it?

No.

The bandage on her arm…that was real.

The throbbing mark on her leg…that was real.

All of it was *very* real.

Steffany didn't feel fear often. Hadn't for a very long time. Yet if what pursued her was what she suspected it was…then she knew why she'd been attacked. Knew why he had come to her house this morning as she was about to sleep.

He knew. *They* knew.

They knew what was going to happen only a few hours from now.

Midnight beckoned.

The dull pain that beat like a drum in time to her heartbeat snared her attention. His touch—the graze of his fingertips—had marked her. Nothing she could do about that now. Didn't matter where she went or what she did, he *would* find her.

It's simply a matter of time.

She yawned. Again. Rubbed at bloodshot eyes.

Tired. Hungry. Thirsty.

Outside, the sun was setting, casting shadows through the mall's glass roof.

It wouldn't be long now. The numbers that provided her safety would gradually diminish. Disperse. The oblivious shoppers would finish crossing all the items off their lists and, pleased with their day's purchases, stroll for the exits, bulging bags in hand. A few would meander home, enjoying a damp but mild evening. Others would amble to the bus stops or train stations where mass transit would ferry them to the destination of their choice. Most, she suspected, would head for the parking lots, and make the trip home secure in their vehicles.

Inside a box of steel and glass, they could lock the doors and be protected.

Would even that stop him?

Steffany *wished* she had a car. Wished she could drive away. Far, far away. But she didn't. She couldn't.

Once all the patrons had left, it would be the staff's turn. They would tidy their stores, roll down the shutters, count up the day's takings, and then revel in their freedom. Saturday night. The shackles of a working week finally removed.

Then where will I go?

Her bare foot bobbed nervously as she nibbled a thumbnail already bitten down so far she could taste the metallic hint of her blood. She could smell it. She didn't care. It would heal quickly enough. Just like the nasty gash on her forearm. A painful souvenir of her desperate escape. Steffany wasn't sure if it was still bleeding. She hadn't taken off the bandages to check.

"You should go to a hospital for that, love," the lady in the pharmacy had advised as she rang up the sunglasses and first aid supplies Steffany had placed on the checkout before handing over the last of the cash she found in her pants with a trembling, bloodstained hand.

No shit, Sherlock!

She was right. Of course she was. But that would lead to questions from receptionists, nurses, and doctors, demanding answers she didn't want to give.

The dark smudges around her eyes told the story of her lack of sleep. It was a choice. A choice to stay alive. Sharp teeth bit into skin again. The pain in her nibbled fingers kept her awake. Kept her alert.

Kept her alive.

Her eyes flicked rapidly from person to person, trying to decipher the clues. The hints that would tell her who was innocent. Who was harmless.

Who was not.

The hard metal bench that had become her temporary refuge was large enough to seat three, and the shopping centre was busy today. Time and again, someone would sit alongside her. Too many times, too many people to tally. In truth, she was too distracted to count. Every time someone sat on her bench, her heart would race. Steffany cast a furtive glance sideways to see who her current companion was. She'd been there a while.

A woman.

Mid-twenties. Maybe. Steffany had always been a terrible judge of age. Silk-like hair cascaded down over her shoulders in fluid ebony waves, contrasting sharply with her perfect complexion. Emerald eyes vivid against pale skin as smooth as porcelain. Utterly perfect. Too perfect. Unblemished. Black jacket. Black pants encased slender legs. Crossed. Black heels perched on dainty feet. Businesswoman, maybe?

Steffany sniffed. A sweet aroma met her nostrils.

Like honey.

The furtive glance became something more. A lingering look. There was something that seemed familiar...

The woman noticed Steffany's scrutiny. She smiled kindly. "Are you all right?" Her English-rose voice was as flawless as her face. A lilting melody as sweet as her scent.

Steffany said nothing.

"Forgive me for noticing, but you've been here a while," the stranger said, her eyes taking in Steffany from her tousled hair to her grubby feet. "I hope you don't mind my saying, but...you look like you're in trouble."

Steffany said nothing.

What *could* she say?

The woman nodded knowingly. She reached a hand across, placing it gently on Steffany's knee. A spark. Steffany flinched at the contact.

"I understand," she said gently.

No, you really don't.

"You should get some sleep."

Steffany didn't fight it. She couldn't. Her eyes drifted slowly closed. As her brain slipped away into the oblivion of much-needed sleep, she thought she heard the woman say one last thing.

"I'll catch up with you later…"

* * *

When Steffany awoke, the sun had surrendered the high ground. Blue skies turned indigo. The moon ascended.

The woman was gone.

She was alone.

Steffany cursed her stupidity.

How long was I asleep?

Late-night shopping was at an end. The centre was closing. Midnight couldn't be far away now.

Panic began to set in as her mind whirled. She had questions with no answers. Where could she go? Where would she be safe?

She wanted to go home but knew that was not an option. Not yet. He'd been there. Broken in. Tried to kill her. The memory surfaced unbidden, making her shake and shudder uncontrollably. She tried to push it away. Shunt it aside. Balling her fists, she screwed her eyes closed.

Think happy thoughts.

She ran her tongue across her teeth. Felt the points of her canines. Lost in a memory.

Vampire.

Of *course* everybody knew what a Vampire was. But they considered them to be an abstract concept. A monster that only existed in storybooks. In TV shows and movies. When you reached out to touch a Vampire, there was supposed to be a wall between you. A glass or plastic screen. The paper on which the words were written.

You couldn't touch them.

They didn't exist.

Steffany knew better.

How surprised would everyone be when they discovered the truth?

That they were real. They were here.

She had been sleeping when the intruder came. Curled up in bed. Safely cocooned in the curtained darkness of her bedroom. She had planned on a quiet day. There was a big, important event coming. She wanted to be rested.

She didn't know how he got in. They had their ways.

At first, she had assumed she was being robbed. Her house being broken into.

He'd have regretted that.

At five-three in bare feet and weighing in at a little over seventy kilos, she was average in size. But she knew she was scrappy. A fighter. She liked to think that was why she'd been given the job at the Ministry of Defence.

But when she felt the strength of the stranger, felt his breath on her neck as he pinned her face down, she had felt true terror for the first time in her long life. She fought back. Pushing and shoving, kicking and lashing out with all her strength. It bought Steffany the tiniest sliver of an opportunity. Room. A window for escape. She took it.

Stumbling down the stairs, the front door was locked. No time to find keys. She dashed into the back room and crashed through the glass of the patio doors. She threw her arms across her face to protect herself from the shattered shards as she fled into the bright early morning sun. Her mind whirling.

They were real. A myth made manifest.

Walking among them undetected.

Unseen.

Her people needed to know.

Surely there would be *something* they could do.

Surely there was a plan for this?

She wished she had her phone. But she had left it. Even now, it was probably sitting idly on her bedside table. Useless to her. Steffany didn't know if he—it—had followed her to the sanctuary of the shopping centre, but there was no way she was going home. She didn't dare return. Not now. Not yet.

No way.

Tomorrow. Tomorrow it would be safe.

Maybe.

The shops were quiet now. Almost empty. The time had come. She couldn't stay any longer.

A thought occurred.

He would come. He would find her. Finish the job before…

Did he know? Did her attacker *know* what was coming? What was planned?

Was she the only one who had been attacked?

Or was this paranoia born from fear and exhaustion?

She froze. Another frantic thought followed as she pursued this new line of inquiry. Things had abruptly taken on a different spin. If her attacker *was* what she feared he was, then she had to suppress her anxiety. Conquer it.

I have to tell someone!

There were no payphones here. Not anymore. They'd disappeared a long time ago. Even if there were, she didn't know the numbers to call. She couldn't remember them. No one did these days. The blessing and the curse of modern technology.

She didn't want to go home, but she had to. There was no longer a choice. Steffany *needed* her phone. She had to call them. Let them know.

She eased herself to her feet and began to pad toward the exit, hoping it wasn't too late.

* * *

Gemma knew she should have played it safe. Taken the well-lit, well-trodden main roads rather than risking the shortcut across the park, through the alleyway, and down the towpath. Yes, she was running late, and yes, it cut almost twenty minutes off her walk to the nightclub, but it was also dingy, wet, and frequented by the homeless. The place reeked of urine and probably worse. There were no lights here. None that worked anyway.

This was a domain of shadows.

And monsters.

Stupid. Stupid. Stupid.

She heard the crunch of the gravel a moment before her attacker was upon her. Before she could react, she found herself sent sprawling by a forceful impact. As she fell, her purse slipped from her grasp. She watched the moonlight glint off its sequined surface as it bounced into the murky waters of the canal. Her knees hit the path first, painfully shredding their skin as the gravel tore at them. Her little black dress tendered little in the way of protection. The palms of her hands came next, sharp stones digging in, giving the painful gift of abrasions that oozed scarlet.

Tears sprang to her eyes, but the pain kept her sane. She wasted no time struggling to crawl away, pleading for her life. Her begging turned to screams as something sharp pierced the soft skin at her back and hip, pinning her in place. Gemma sobbed, secure in the knowledge something truly horrifying was about to happen to her amongst the piss-stained trash.

Her only option was to fight.

She kicked out. Twisting and writhing, searching for any leverage to escape.

She looked up, expecting to see the face of the man who attacked her. Who had stabbed her.

But it wasn't a man.

Gemma was shocked to see her assailant was a barefoot young woman. Smaller, shorter, slighter than her, yet stronger. Much stronger. Veins bulged in her neck and one uncovered forearm. The other was wrapped in a loose and bloody bandage. There were no knives. Her assailant's fingers were long—far too long to be normal—and tipped in curved, razor-sharp talons that dripped a thick, dark liquid.

Gemma's blood.

Yet, as unexpectedly terrifying as that was, it was the face that held her complete attention.

Furious eyes burned beneath the severe arch of an angry brow. Wide black pupils filled irises so pale they appeared to blend into the whites. Her face was unnaturally contorted by a wide mouth. Distended almost. A chilling quartet of sharp teeth that both fascinated and horrified Gemma gleamed in what scant light was available on the dark canal side. A pair of smaller points on the lower jaw mirrored by long curved canines—fangs—dripped with something.

Blood maybe?

Something else?

Vampire.

The word thudded through her mind with every rapid beat of her terrified heart.

What else could this creature possibly be?

"Stop." A voice cut through the night. Strong. Authoritative.

Her assailant froze.

Gemma craned her head to look. A woman. Tall and willowy. Well dressed. Tailored black pantsuit. She seemed to shimmer and glow, illuminating the towpath around her. Perfect skin and long flowing ebony hair. Beautiful.

An angel?

The vampire's claw corkscrewed into her shoulder, pressing her down to the pavement. Gemma whimpered, but twisted, fighting back. Rolling over, she reached up and raked the face of her attacker with her own nails. False nails. She'd never been able to grow her own. They broke easily but did the job. The monster shrieked, briefly relinquishing her grip and pulling away as Gemma sought to dig the broken plastic into those pale eyes. Anything to keep the monster's attention on her. To give the stranger a chance to escape the same fate that was likely to befall her.

She might die here tonight, but nobody else needed to.

Especially not an angel.

"Run!" Gemma called out weakly. "Run!"

Yet out of the corner of her eye, she saw the stranger continue her approach.

Why? Please, run while you have the chance!

"You found me!" The Vampire suddenly sounded...afraid?

"Taking refuge in the shopping centre was a nice touch. Hiding amongst the humans," the woman said. "But the truth is, I marked you with magic the moment I found you in your home. There was no hiding from me."

"From *you*? But I thought..." The Vampire's fear was now shaded with confusion.

The stranger's face changed, smoothly shifting from female to male where it lingered for a moment.

There was a brief look of shock on the Vampire's expression as realisation dawned and her tone changed. "It *was* you. Of course it was you. Male, female, whatever. It's all the same to you shapeshifters, isn't it?"

Changing back to the familiar female face again, her expression never wavered. "Shifting forms allowed me to get close to you again—

"You put me to sleep," the Vampire interrupted, nodding her understanding.

"I couldn't attack you with all those people around, but I needed to neutraliseneutralize you as a threat. I knew you'd run again at nightfall. All I had to do was get you away from there without any drama," the stranger explained. "It's over now. So why don't you step *away* from the girl, Steffany."

"You know my name?"

"We know a lot of things, Steffany of House Jareb."

It sounded like a flex. A subtle hint regarding just how much the stranger knew. Gemma didn't understand the reference, but apparently, the Vampire did.

"Then you know it's not over," Steffany retorted. "You *know* what's coming."

The stranger nodded. "We do. And it *does* end now. You caught us with our guard down in America—"

"And everywhere else," Steffany scoffed.

"But Europe is a different matter. We *won't* let it fall."

"Like you'll have a choice," Steffany growled as she tossed Gemma aside and began to stalk toward the ebony-haired woman. "We've been planning this for *years*. Preparing. Seeding ourselves amongst humanity and their institutions of power."

"Like the Ministry of Defence, Steffany? Right and wrong—there's always a choice. Even for a Vampyrii. And right now, you're making a bad one."

"Am I?" Steffany retorted. "We're through being afraid of you. Of humanity. It's kill or be killed, right?"

Gemma wanted to close her eyes. But she didn't.

She didn't want to witness the beast with the fangs and claws tearing this brave stranger apart. But she couldn't turn away. Was it simply a dreadful fascination? Or morbid curiosity regarding what might happen to her next?

Either way, Gemma stared in wide-eyed terror as the monster approached her latest victim.

Yet the stranger showed no fear in the face of such fanged ferocity.

She didn't move.

Didn't run.

Instead, she rose gracefully into the air, her feet leaving the ground as a breeze kicked up around her. It grew quickly in strength, sweeping down the towpath and rippling the calm waters of the canal. Her fingers curled abstractly as she started to move her arms in arcane patterns. Her hair whipped around her face.

What is happening?

A memory surfaced. Gemma as a little girl, putting her head out of the car window as her father drove along the road. Faster and faster. The wind in her hair, pressure against her face.

Squinting against the gale, she stared at the stranger.

Gemma's jaw slackened. Her mouth dropped open.

The stranger was the centre of the storm.

Trash of all varieties was swept up. Discarded newspapers and crisp packets danced and whirled in the vortex she was creating. With a flick of her wrists, the wind altered course, battering the advancing Vampire who pushed forward, struggling against the intense resistance. Fighting against the raging maelstrom. Each plodding step was accompanied by an angry snarl. Lethal hands strained, reaching toward the stranger with talon-tipped menace.

Then something struck the Vampire in the chest.

Then another something.

Then a third.

The projectiles began to come thick and fast, physically pounding the monster's torso. Each impact tore clothing and drew blood before clattering to the pavement where Gemma could finally see them.

Stones.

Jagged black stones the size of tennis balls lay on the footpath, smouldering.

Why are they smouldering?

One rolled close to Gemma. She stretched out a curious hand to pick it up but dropped it just as quickly. It was hot. Very hot. Like a coal from a fireplace.

The Vampire ceased her advance, turned her head aside, and lifted her arms to protect her face from the onslaught.

The wind subsided.

"Stop this now. While you still can, Vampyrii," the woman ordered. "I'm *not* here to kill you. Simply to neutralize you. I can't let you go to the Ministry tomorrow. Walk away now. Hide. Forsake your role in what is to come. Because if you continue to resist, if you continue on this course—"

"Kill me if you like, Fae," Steffany angrily spat back at her. "It doesn't matter. If the legends are true, then you are few. We are *legion*. And we are already *everywhere*. So, strike me down. Someone will take my place and do what must be done. At midnight it begins."

Fae? Did she say Fae?

"Then why this one?" the Fae asked. "Starting a little early?"

The monster shrugged. "I always was eager to get started. This day has been a long time coming. Too long. Crawl back to whatever hole you've been hiding in for all these centuries. This is none of your concern. Not anymore."

"No." The Fae shook her head. "We're not hiding anymore. Never again. We tried to let you live in peace, but you're forcing our hand."

"Then do your worst," the Vampyrii growled.

She did.

Not with the wind this time. Not with stone.

With fire.

The breeze picked up again, but now it felt…different.

The oxygen Gemma was breathing felt fresher. Richer. Purer. She suddenly felt wide awake. Alert and euphoric.

Her eyes were transfixed by the floating Fae as she thrust her hands toward the Vampire, wrists together, palms outward, fingers outstretched and slightly curled. A narrow jet of flame shot out, streaming across the distance between them. The monster was engulfed. Enveloped by a raging inferno that covered every inch of her body with rampant dancing flames. Gemma scrambled backward, lifting one bloody hand to protect herself from the almost unbearable heat while the other grabbed at the tiny silver crucifix on the chain around her neck.

Gemma wanted to look away. She had no desire to watch a young woman burn to death, no matter what kind of monster she really was. But she couldn't. Her eyes were transfixed, witnessing something she would never, ever forget.

The Vampire screamed.

Gemma screamed. Hers lasted longer. Hers didn't die on charred lips.

The Vampire dropped first to her knees, then slumped slowly forward. Her still-burning body hit the ground with a hollow thud, patches of charred skin flaking off, and lay still.

Deathly still.

The wind dissipated gradually as a small shower of rain appeared from nowhere directly above them. The mini deluge soaked Gemma while dowsing the flames that still crackled and spit on the fallen Vampire. The smell was a mixture of burnt hair and cooked meat. Gemma couldn't help but think of a barbecue…

…and how she never wanted to go to one again.

The thought unsettled Gemma's already churning stomach, and she could feel the bile rising. Burning her throat. She scrambled urgently to the side of the canal and vomited into the water until her ribs hurt. Her body was shaking uncontrollably. Shock. Cold. She couldn't stop sobbing with relief.

She was alive.

Cold, bedraggled, bloodied, and bruised. But most importantly, *alive*.

The Fae woman drifted toward her before touching down gracefully a few meters away. She walked the rest of the way, the gravel of the path barely whispering at her passage. When she got to Gemma, she bent slightly and offered an elegant hand. Gemma stared at it hesitantly.

"Are you really…Fae?" Her voice came out a broken croak.

The woman nodded.

"Is it…is it over?"

The answer was at first a relief. "For now."

Yet as the words sank in, Gemma realisedrealized what it truly meant. That the immediate danger had passed, but this wasn't the end of it.

Gemma accepted the offered hand and climbed gingerly to her feet. The heel of one of her shoes was broken, causing her to stand lopsidedly. Her dress was torn, ruined. Water dripped rhythmically from her hair. She shivered.

"Thank you," she stammered.

"It was my duty," the stranger said cryptically. "You're hurt. Here…"

Gentle fingers brushed across the slashes the Vampire's claws had left. The memory of the wounds seemed to conjure the forgotten pain. Gemma winced. But a moment later, as the tender touch became a firm press of the Fae's palm, the agony was soothed. When the hand was removed, Gemma peered at the spot on her shoulder where her flesh had been pierced.

The blood remained, but the wound was healed.

"How?" she stammered.

The woman shrugged and smiled as she took Gemma's bloody hands into her own. "Magic," she said simply.

Once she was done fixing Gemma's wounds, the Fae woman turned to the canal. Her fingers danced and swirled in the air. A number of rippling water tentacles rose and twisted toward them. Several reached for the blackened Vampire corpse, curling around it and hauling it over the edge of the embankment where it fell into the murky waters with a gentle splash. It disappeared beneath the waters, leaving no trace it had ever been there.

Another tentacle stretched out toward Gemma, and for a moment, she feared that she, too, was about to be dragged into the shallow depths of the canal. But then she noticed that at the tip was a purse she recognized.

Black with silver sparkles. Bought to match her dress.

The Fae plucked it from the air as the tentacle fell back into the waterway. She handed it to Gemma who tentatively accepted it.

She nodded toward the water. "Won't she…it…be missed?"

The woman shook her head. "I doubt it. Not until it's too late, anyway."

"Thank you," she whispered again. "For everything."

"Go home," the Fae woman said. "And stay there."

Gemma wasn't sure if it was advice or a warning. Perhaps both.

Regardless, it wasn't enough to explain what happened here tonight. She needed more. She needed answers to put what she had just witnessed into context. To decipher the words she just heard.

'At midnight it begins,' the Vampire had said.

'Not until it's too late,' her saviour had just said.

What did that mean?

"Wait! Who…are you?" Gemma stammered. "What was… What's going on? What's all this about?"

The woman stopped. Looked back. "My name is Serlia. There is a war coming. A rising," she said. "It won't last long. Go home. Hurry. Tell your family. Tell your friends. Hide. Find somewhere safe."

ABOUT THE AUTHOR

Jon Ford lives in Worcestershire, UK.

He lives with his awesome Wifey, their lovable puppy, Vixen, and the demonic hell-puppy, Lyssa. All of them live under the watchful gaze of their cat-overlords Lana and Gale.

No awards to brag about, but he's working on it.

Currently writing two series of books.

The Ballad of the Songbird is an urban fantasy saga with sci-fi overtones. Book 1 'Hunters' and book 2 'Blood to Earth' are out now. Book 3 'Tooth & Claw' will be in mid-2023.

The Femme Fatales is an ongoing sci-fi superhero series. Book 1 'The Scorched Sky' and a tie-in novella 'Knightingale' is out now. Book 2 'The Broken Ground' will be out later in 2023.

To find out more about either series - and for my random musings - please visit and explore my expansive website:

WWW.JONFORDAUTHOR.COM

Co-Founder of Tepris Press with NT Anderson.

A little indie imprint label dedicated to putting out high-quality independent books.

Find out more at our website:

WWW.TEPRISPRESS.COM

Also, find me on Twitter at: @_Knightingale

And on Instagram at: JonFordAuthor

Demontia

Halo Scot

*T*rust. A slimy thing. Easy to lose, tough to find. And in a city of thousands, it was extinct.

Gio Luca trusted no one. He grew up with all the right things but all the wrong people. Car for his birthday, guilt from his grades. Fund for his future, shame from his past. He acted out to break in, but he felt nothing despite all the chaos he caused.

The neighbors called him troubled. His family called him difficult. Gio called himself done, so he lit trash on fire and spray-painted brownstones. He was on a first-name basis with Boston Police Department. They never kept him long; Gio had money, and money was freedom. Cash turned the tightest prudes into whores.

Gio started as a bad boy: theft, drugs, fucking everything that moved. Bad boys were cool. But now, he was a bad man, and that was no longer cool.

"When are you gonna do something with your life?" his aunt asked.

Gio hated this question. He was doing plenty with his life, just not what she wanted. "Soon, Zia Rosa."

Patrons stuffed into the tiny trattoria. Conversations buzzed in a mix of Italian and English. Gio slurped spaghetti off a fork and earned Rosa's wrinkled disgust. Twilight shone through arched windows, casting his aunt in severe shadows: crow-black curls, hazel eyes, high cheekbones, olive skin. Gio shared these features. His whole family did. They were clones, though Gio was sharper, meaner, carved from concrete and cut from steel. He wouldn't entertain these disparaging meals if his aunt didn't hold the family's purse strings. She didn't hold them tightly, though. For that, Gio was relieved if not grateful, but Rosa did it for his cousins, not for him. She made it fair, even if Gio didn't deserve fair.

"Gio," Zia Rosa scolded.

Gio leaned against the brick wall, prepared for her verbal attack.

His aunt sucked in a spittle-soaked breath that tortured the candles before it tortured him. "You're not a child anymore. When I was your age, I had three jobs and five kids."

And of those five kids, three rotted in prison, one was wanted in four states, and the last struggled to hold down any job with her shoplifting fetish. Yes, we were all so proud.

"I got a few things in motion," Gio said. Nothing the family would approve, but Gio valued his defiance. It was the one thing he could control.

"Off you go, then." His aunt stole his plate and shooed Gio away. "Do something useful. Get a job."

But Gio was happy living off his trust fund. Jobs were boring. Everyone told him so. They were excuses to complain and buy liquor on weekdays.

"Later, Zia," Gio said. He kissed his aunt's cheek, shrugged on his leather jacket, and left the trattoria.

Yes, Gio went, but he did not do something useful. Nor did he get a job. Instead, he walked through the North End, aimless, scowling at the chill. Skeletal branches cradled the ghostly moon, peeking over roofs of red-brick buildings. Crowds swarmed the slim, tangled streets. This was a walking neighborhood, even on freeze-your-balls-off nights like tonight. Gio passed cafes, pizzerias, trattorias, quaint stores, and luxury restaurants. The Italian flag flew outside most shops. This was Little Italy, the motherland wrenched across the ocean in the sixteen hundreds. It was old and cold, small and steep. You'd be hard-pressed to find a house less than a million on the peninsula. Lucky for Gio, a million was no problem. His family's financial empire paid for all his unsavory exploits.

An ice-edged gust spiked through Gio's jacket, and he swore in two languages. Late fall in Boston was the Devil's playground: windy, wild, frigid, a breeding ground for myth. Gio believed in myth, in magic, though his family thought him insane. As a kid, he shared these beliefs, but no longer. Magic was precious, a treasure he kept for himself, tucked away in a pocket of memory.

Gio's phone buzzed in his pocket. He cursed his massive family. There was always a problem or some gossip. Drama gnawed at every interaction. He considered ignoring it, but Nonna was in the hospital. Zia Rosa would tear him a new one if he missed an important call. "She could die any day," his aunt always said… and she'd been saying it for the past two decades. Nonna was stubborn as a mule. She would die on her terms, and on her terms only. Today was not that day.

Reluctant, Gio answered, "Hey."

His father's voice scratched across the line. "Get to the hospital. Nonna's taken a turn. Today, she forgot Uncle Marco."

Gio tried to be gentle—as gentle as a dagger could be. "She has dementia. She forgets someone every day." And in a family this large, Gio couldn't blame her. He wished he could forget half of them.

His father's sigh rivaled the wind, and Gio shivered inside his jacket. "Gio Antonio Francesco Luca"—Gio winced at the Italian artillery—"get your ass down here *now*. Nonna thinks she's been cursed."

Gio muted the call to hide his snort. Italians feared a mountain of superstitions: the number seventeen, black cats, table corners, hats on beds, sweeping feet, broken mirrors, opening umbrellas indoors, spilling olive oil, et cetera, ad infinitum. Gio found their fear ironic. His family didn't believe in magic, but they believed in curses—which were the same thing, if you asked Gio. Problem was, no one asked Gio.

Off mute, Gio said, "Dad, chill. She's not cursed, and she's not dying. I'm busy tonight."

"You ungrateful sh—"

Gio heard his mother take the phone. "What your father means, darling, is if you don't visit Nonna now, the next time you visit her, she might not be Nonna. Memories make a person."

A line pirated from one of her favorite dramedies.

"She forgot me first," Gio said. "It won't make a difference."

"It might help her remember," his mom said. "Please, Gio. All your sisters and brothers are here."

All nine of them, Gio was sure. A joy for the hospital staff, no doubt. "I went last Sunday, after she hit her head. It didn't help. If she can't remember me, she won't miss me. Gotta go."

Gio cut the call. His dad would give him shit for it later, but he didn't plan on being around later. He ducked down a side alley and quickened his pace. Family stress always made him want to lash out, and Copp's Hill Burying Ground was the perfect place to release some well-honed rage.

Night fell fast and brutal, the swing of an ax from practiced hands. Gio reached the cemetery as darkness thickened into an inky blanket. Flashlights pierced this blanket, and he grinned as he found his friends. Well, not friends, but they didn't hate him, so Gio counted them in the green.

"Gio, you moody fuck." Leo slapped his back with the force of a freight train, and Gio swallowed blood from his bitten tongue. "Let's wreck some shit."

Dante and Viv joined them, their quartet complete, all the troubled kids who became troubled adults, society's barfed-up rejects. Yes, they had rage in spades. Leo handed them all baseball bats, and they got to work.

This was how they had all met five years ago—smashing graves, robbing coffins. Fate (or the Devil) had brought them together, and they had terrorized Boston's corpses for half a decade. The cops had busted them from most cemeteries in the city, so this was their last jaunt. Gio didn't like vandalizing in his own neighborhood—it was like shitting in your own garden—but fertilizer was fertilizer, so he watched chaos grow.

They destroyed in silence for an hour. Bats sliced the autumn chill, and graves cracked into pieces, a stone city of shattered memories. Gio believed things hid in these cracks. He thought cracks in graves, in death, led to cracks in reality, and that these cracks in reality sheltered lost hope and forgotten dreams. However, nobody else thought this, and after years of ruining graveyards, Gio had yet to suffer anything more than a mild arrest.

When his parents found out about his nighttime hobby, they were furious. "Cemeteries are cursed," they'd said. "If you go after dark, they steal something from you."

Of course cemeteries were cursed. Everything was cursed. Curses were reasons to shirk responsibility. For a family as wealthy as his, they coveted laziness—a trait Gio inherited with pleasure, his sole claim to the Luca name.

Rock shards pelted his cheek. He glared in their direction, and Viv winked a slate-gray eye. She was the most destructive of them, with a record longer than all theirs combined. In truth, she scared Gio, though he'd never admit it. She always escalated their games into all-out wars.

"I got some gasoline," Viv said, tossing a dark braid over her shoulder. "Wanna have some fun?"

Gio eyed her low-cut dress with a different idea of fun, but Viv's fun needed to come before anyone else's fun—pun intended.

"Sure," Gio said.

Viv poured gasoline over a bouquet of trampled lilies. There was a symbol there, one Gio was too horny to find. He removed a match from his pocket, lit the end, and tossed it at the flowers. Nothing happened. The fire blinked out.

"Are you sure that's gas?" Dante asked, amused.

"Unlike you, I'm not an idiot," Viv snapped.

She poured more gas over the flowers and motioned for another match. Gio lit a second one, threw it, but darkness again swallowed the flame. Smoke swirled from the defeated match.

"Losing your touch, Viv," Leo teased.

Gio knew Viv was not, in fact, losing any sort of touch, but he didn't mention this to Leo. No one knew about his and Viv's relationship... though "relationship" wasn't the right term. They weren't lovers or fuck buddies or friends with benefits. They were two lonely people who were sometimes the things that went bump in the night.

Sirens cried nearby. The four not-friends gathered their bats and ran. Then the sirens disappeared, and they disappeared, too.

* * *

Darkness drowned the cemetery.

Gio couldn't see—their flashlights didn't work—but he could hear Leo's heavy breaths. Dante hummed, pretending away fear, and Viv clasped Gio's hand, since it was dark as grief. Gio was not afraid. He wasn't particularly attached to life, so death carried little threat. Still, he squeezed Viv's fingers and pulled her close, comforting her through muscle memory if not kindness. It wasn't that he didn't care about her; it was that he didn't care about himself.

"Anyone there?" Leo shouted, voice shaking. Gio heard a baseball bat swing through the darkness, then a fleshy thump.

"Ouch, you asshole," Dante said. "Watch it."

"You watch it. There's something out there."

"There's nothing out there," Gio said. "It's a blackout, that's all. Let's walk, and I'm sure we'll find the road."

They didn't have a chance to walk, and life once again proved Gio wrong.

"Another Luca," an oily whisper slithered from the shadows.

A scrape of moonlight emerged from the darkness. It morphed into the shape of a woman, unveiling the terror on Gio's not-friends' faces. Her glowing body wriggled with legions of maggots, slugs, and albino snakes. Razored bones and crumpled cartilage pierced her wormy frame. Twin tarantulas posed as eyes in her writhing skull. A fanged maw opened above her chin, and she laughed the scratch of swords on ice.

Leo squealed. Dante pissed himself. Viv seized in Gio's arms. Gio waited for fear, but again, it didn't come. Awe did, though. Awe and wonder. As the monstrous woman approached them, her body illuminated the space. No graves, no grass, no trees, no Boston. The world was shadow, midnight fog and an empty sky. Gio knew where they were: a crack in reality.

The woman chuckled. "Smarter than others think, aren't you, Gio? But you like being underestimated. Keeps expectations low. Then you don't need to push yourself."

Gio released Viv as the woman's light reached them. Leo whimpered, and Dante pissed himself again. Gio did neither.

"Who are you?" he asked.

The woman stretched a scaly, squirming hand toward Gio and trailed a talon down his cheek. Blood wept from the gash, but Gio didn't move. At last, he felt something, and he'd choose pain over nothing any day of the week.

"You could call me a family friend," the monster hissed. "Your grandmother and I were rather close."

Gio stifled his surprise. Nonna was a saint—a feisty saint, but a saint all the same. She dreaded everything related to the supernatural and wouldn't be caught dead with a… whatever this woman was.

"You know what I am. Say it." The serpentine woman slapped his wrist, crushing bone. Pain exploded up Gio's arm. He collapsed to the wispy ground as his not-friends screeched and sobbed. None of them helped him. They were too mortified.

Gio remembered the myth most forgot. "Demon… demontia," he spit.

"Dementia?" Dante asked.

"De*mon*tia," the demon sneered, "though we're the reason for your word. Humans were too afraid to keep the original root: demon. Your species has always been too afraid to keep anything of worth."

"You… you're a… demon?" Leo asked, always ten steps behind.

"Yes," the woman said, "but don't blame me for your misfortune. *You* summoned *me*."

"S-s-summoned-d?" Dante stuttered.

"With a sacrifice of stone and smoke."

The graves and matches, Gio thought.

"Don't you know the legends?" the demon asked.

Leo, Dante, and Viv shook their heads. Gio remained silent, crippled by pain.

The demon rolled her tarantula eyes, and a wet squelch sounded as she refocused on them. "You should. Gio does. His grandmother does, too. She summoned me with rosary beads and cigarettes. Give her my regards, if you remember."

A wicked smile squished her wiggly features as she turned toward Gio.

"She was in that graveyard because of you," the demon continued, "praying for her troubled grandson under a full moon. She worried about you. Wanted you to find a better path. Thought the bad road would end if she asked for divine intervention. Problem was, divinity was preoccupied, but demons always have time on their hands." She grabbed Gio's hair and yanked back his head. "It's your fault, Gio Luca. That's why I stole you first."

"Stole him?" Leo asked, ashen.

Gio urged as much dignity into his voice as he could while on his knees, manhandled by a demon. "She stole Nonna's memory of me."

The demon again smiled, and Gio trembled in her grip, horror finally rooting in his bones. "Your grandmother would do anything to save her family, and so would I."

She released Gio, greasy arms rising at her sides. Dozens of pale creatures slid through the shadows, all as grotesque and grisly as her. Bodies full of maggots and worms. Bone spikes and spider eyes. They crawled on all fours, drooling and groaning. Here, Gio allowed himself a shriek.

"Now, you understand," the demon woman said. "And please accept our sincere apology. We need loneliness to breed, and memory theft spawns such delicious desolation. There is nothing worse than forgetting you are loved. We aren't greedy, though. Every night, we'll erase one person from your mind, until they're all gone. With a family as large as yours, Gio, you'll have plenty of time before you lose everyone. Your friends, though, won't have such luck."

The demon opened her maw and kissed Gio's temple while three of her family did the same to Leo, Dante, and Viv. Gio gagged as her soggy tongue stabbed his skull, gliding into his brain with a crackling burst of agony. He tried to scream, but pain consumed him. A thousand needles punctured his mind, white-hot and razor-sharp. With a visceral rip, the demon tore a bundle of memories from him. A woman's silhouette faded—someone he used to know and could have cared about if he allowed himself to care.

The tongue slid free of Gio's skull. Blood gushed from the wound.

"You should have visited your grandmother," the demon said. "If you had, we never would have met. Then again, in a way, we haven't. You won't remember me. Soon, you'll remember no one."

Fresh agony crashed over Gio. He buckled beneath its might and crumpled on the shadowy ground. Darkness ate him as he howled, undone.

* * *

Steady beeps and a sterile sting woke Gio.

He blinked heavy eyelids and peered at the fluorescent ceiling. A hospital, then. Gio knew all hospitals in the Boston area from his rebellious phase... a phase that had lasted since birth.

"What the hell happened last night?" his father demanded from his bedside.

"Tony, stop. Give him a minute." His mother's gentle touch warmed Gio's arm. Comfort was a trap. "The cops found you beaten on Copp's Hill with a few other people. Did they do this to you?"

Gio remembered nothing since the grave smashing, but his not-friends wouldn't hurt him like this. He shook his head; the movement sent a cascade of pain through his mind. He almost blacked out, but held on with a thready breath.

What the hell *had* happened last night? Did they drink? Smoke? Snort? Shoot up? All Gio knew was he had a skull-splitting headache, and his body felt like someone had shoved lava in every joint.

"Then what happened, Gio?" his mother asked, impatient. "You annoyed Rosa, avoided Nonna, ran off to God knows where—"

Gio was sure God had nothing to do with it.

"—and showed up here with a crushed wrist and a hole in your temple, not to mention that dreadful gash." She tapped the stitches on his cheek, and he bit back a gasp.

"I can't remember, Mom," Gio said. "Sorry."

"You're not sorry. You're never sorry, and I'm sick of your bullshit." His mom was not gentle anymore. "Get your act together, Gio, or you're cut off."

It wasn't the first time she threatened to cut him off, and it wouldn't be the last. Gio didn't worry. She'd calm down. His dad, too. They were all bark, which was why Gio was a spoiled, messed-up, delinquent asshole.

"Anyway," his mom said, scrubbing her face, "there's someone here to see you. We'll be across the hall with Nonna."

His parents left the hospital room, and a woman in a low-cut dress replaced them. Gio didn't know what he had done to deserve her company, but he never questioned fate when fate handed him gold. In retrospect, he should have questioned fate more often.

"Hey, Gio," the woman said. She sunk into a chair and hung her head in her hands. "I have the worst fucking headache." Gio noticed she also had a hole in her skull, stitched together like his. "What the fuck happened last night?"

Gio squinted at her. She knew him, but he didn't know her—and she was someone he would have remembered. "I think you have the wrong room."

The woman quirked her dark brow, gray eyes wide. "Gio, it's me." She tugged her messy braid, nervous. "We've known each other for years."

"We've never met. Sorry, wish we had."

Tears bubbled in her gaze. She balled her hands into fists as frustration shook her arms. "I don't know what game you're playing, but it's bullshit. You can act all tough with Dante and Leo, but don't be a dumbass with me. We didn't share much, but we shared something, and I won't be another of your throwaway girls."

Gio remembered Dante and Leo. They weren't close, but they were useful. Chaos was a group activity. He still didn't remember this woman, though.

"I hit my head last night," Gio said, pointing at his temple. "What's your name? Maybe it'll jog my memory."

The woman's cheeks reddened, and she spit in his face. "Fucking asshole." Then she stormed from the room, and Gio wiped phlegm from his eye, confused.

His father's voice drifted through the hallway. "Ma, it's Tony. You know me."

"Maria, get this man out of my room," Nonna croaked.

"He's your son," Gio's mother said. "Please, try to remember."

"I've never seen him in my life. Get him away."

A nurse closed Gio's door with a sympathetic frown. Nonna's protests faded to silence.

"Feeling all right, Gio?" the nurse asked.

"All right enough." Gio learned young that no one wanted the truth, especially if it meant more work for them.

"Great. Why don't you get some rest, and I'll check on you in a few hours?"

"Sure." Gio closed his eyes as the nurse shut off the lights and left.

An uneasy feeling wormed its way into his mind: pale and slimy, soggy and grotesque. Gio couldn't help thinking there was something—or a lot of somethings—he should remember. But he was exhausted, and his head pounded with his pulse, a drumbeat of agony tempting him into the abyss. Shadows wrapped him in their tendrils and dragged him into nightmare.

Before he fell, Gio thought he heard greasy rustles and an oily whisper.

Tonight, we'll steal another.

ABOUT THE AUTHOR

Halo Scot is a dark fiction author of book monsters, many of which bite. Reviews and press are available on http://HaloScot.com. Halo has been featured in Publishers Weekly and BookLife. Also, as a founding member of http://QueerIndie.com, Scot has appeared at Brooklyn Book Festival and Pop Pride Week, an event hosted by ReedPop, BookCon, and New York Comic Con.

Halo pretends to be cool, dark, and mysterious, when in reality, Scot is a clumsy and awkward creature who eats shadows and harbors a severe distrust of ladybugs. Prone to chaos, this nightmare-dwelling beast aims to achieve galactic domination through a void-screaming expertise, dormant telekinesis, and aggressive cackling. To summon this obscure and skittish writer, one must align the following items in a circle as an offering: three shots of whiskey, two bowls of jelly beans, something shiny or lit on fire, and a printed photo of Nicolas Cage as a duck.

Ginny the Witch Grants a Wish

Chris Hooley

You finish your pint and throw a glare at the men at the end of the bar – they're laughing uncontrollably, and you caused their amusement. Yet again. You're Mr. Loser.

'I don't know why I bother coming to this place,' you say.

The men look at one another, all three of them, and laugh harder. The tallest of them laughs so hard that he coughs. His cough brings the laughter to a natural end and all eyes fall on you, again. They watch as you rise from your bar stool and walk towards the door.

Fed up with being the butt of the joke. Goodbye forever, cocksuckers. You're not a forty-year-old virgin and you know it. You don't need to prove it to them or anyone else, but their laughter still hurts. Their laughter bubbles under your skin and it makes you scratch the back of your neck. Blunt fingernails or not.

'We're just joshing with you. Don't run home to your mummy, just yet.' says the barman, trying to contain another round of laughter.

'Fuck you, Steve. There are other pubs you know.' Leaves your lips.

An old man, much too old to remember his own birthday, has been watching the three fools torment you about your lack of female companion-ship for over an hour.

Just watching and waiting.

It is a good time for him to say his piece. He'd tossed the idea around his mind long enough. He felt sorry for you, but he wasn't sure if his was the best advice to give. It hadn't done him any favours. Everyone he ever loved had died and then died again and again. And he stayed forever 'young'. Forever lonely was more like it. She certainly gave him what he wanted, but that was a mistake. Maybe things will work out differently for you, he thinks.

There was only one way to know for sure.

'Excuse me young'un, you could always see Ginny the Witch. She'd be able to help you with your little lady problems. It would cost you a great deal, but she could definitely help you. She lives at the top of Hilldale in the purple house. You know the one?'

You know the one. It's the creepy arse house, the one you always quicken your pace at. You're Mr. Scaredy-Cat.

The group's chorus of laughter starts again.

'Yeah, see Ginny the Witch. That's the only way you're ever getting laid.'

You don't know which of the three-headed torment monster it is who spits out that line because you're already leaving. The door closes behind you as you feel the first few drops of rain hit your face. It must be raining. You wouldn't cry because of those arseholes, would you? Ginny the Witch. As the thought flows through your mind, your left thumb throbs. That brief pulse is trying to communicate something beyond understanding. Ba bum. Ba bum.

You put your hands in your pockets and head home.

You're Mr. Cry Baby.

Mr. Piss-Wet-Through.

Mr. Lonely.

You sit in your house, and you hear their words circling like sharks in your mind. Snap. Snap. Their jaws lashing at the last ounce of confidence that's left. It's a feeding frenzy. They tear it between them. Their jaws pulling and tearing that last strip of hope like a moist tissue. Why doesn't anyone want to fuck you? Is it because you use phrases like 'fuck you' instead of 'make love to you'? If you had an 'I-can-make-love to-you-face', would that get you anywhere? Is it because you don't have any good chat-up lines? Should you Google some?

'Hey, Siri… give me some good chat-up lines.'

I AM NOT SURE I UNDERSTAND.

'… No, me neither.'

If the internet can't even help you maybe, you should try the purple house. Maybe Ginny the Witch thinks you're fuckable. Maybe she has needs too. A lonely woman in an isolated house in the arsehole of nowhere. Slim pickings all round. Maybe you could feast on each other's bodies like ravenous wolves. You feel a tingling sensation in your pants, and it forces you into action. You stand up and look around at your life.

Everything is neat and exactly how it should be. Nobody has left their cup out on the side for you to clean because there is nobody. There has been no one other than you for as long as you care to remember. You've been Mr. Goatee, Mr. Full-beard, Mr. Moustache, Mr. Bald, Mr. Short-back-and-sides, and even Mr. Perm since the last time you awoke to a stranger in your bed. You're going to that house.

* * *

The Ring doorbell looks out of place on the doorframe of the house which looks as old as time itself. The blue light flashes and you want to run, but you're Mr. Loner and that needs to change, so you wait it out. It's about as comfortable as the time you impaled your nutsack on a speared fence, whilst trying to be 'Tyler Durden' and break into that chemical waste plant. All your 'friends' laughing their heads off as they left you out to dry on the top like a rotisserie chicken, only the freezing, fearful, and yelling in pain type.

'Hello…'

The cackle in her voice sends a shiver up your spine, but you want to be Mr. Brave and he doesn't get scared by elderly women who have a reputation for witchcraft and have strange symbols carved above their doors. You run your finger over the six-lobed flower pattern.

'Don't touch my house! What are you even doing here?'

Your finger snaps back. The brain fog stops you from responding. You just stare at the blue ring. This was a mistake.

'Are you Ginny the Witch?'

'You know I am or else you wouldn't be here! Cut to it. What do you want?'

Mr. Brave. Mr. Brave. Channel that energy. You place your hands into the power stance - thumbs at the top of the diamond, first two fingers touching. The invisible diamond of power is in your hands. Nothing can hurt you. Mr. Gets-Shit-Done.

'I want all women to fall madly in love with me whenever they lay eyes on me.'

The very notion of saying it aloud makes your face crumple into awkwardness. What were you thinking? You better look over your shoulder to make sure nobody heard you say that. You look over your shoulder and the coast is clear. Not even a bird warming on a pylon. You are Mr. Lucky today.

'Interesting. Have you thought about working out more? Being nice? Getting a colonic?'

Your buttocks clench as your hand reaches around at the horror of the suggestion. Mr. Lucky meet Mrs. Invade-Your-Personal-Space.

'No! Listen, I'm not here for you to take the piss. I've had enough of that already. Can you help me or not?'

If a bird was warming on a pylon, they'd have flown off at this pathetic display.

'Sure. It'll cost you one thumb. Just pop one through the hole in the door and your wish is my command.'

The hole in the door reveals itself. It wasn't there before. You would have noticed it, wouldn't you? It's a perfectly thumb-sized hole. It's not a mouth, but it's mouth-like only without teeth. Dark and seemingly as vast as space. The thought of putting your thumb in the hole causes both of your thumbs to retract and hide for cover in the palms of your hands.

'A thumb? Like my actual thumb? Can't I just pay you or something? I have money.'

'Now who's taking the piss? I'm a witch, I don't need money. You want women to fall madly in love with you, and I need a thumb before the next full moon, well I need two actually, but that's not your problem. I think it's a fair trade. Take it or leave it. Going once!'

Left or right. Right or left.

'Going twice!'

You thrust your left thumb into the hole. For a moment, nothing happens.

Then the pain hits your eyes. A flash of light makes you try to pull your thumb back from the hole, but the process has already begun. The grip is so tight; you struggle to breathe. The lack of oxygen to your brain forces you back to a nightmare. Only this wasn't a nightmare. It was real. Remember? That time you got your head stuck in a metal fence and the fire brigade had to set you free… well, the panic you felt at that moment is back and it's been waiting to tear into you for nearly thirty years. You'd scream if the terror of trying to escape your thoughts would stop for even a split second.

Then it stops.

The pain. The memories. Everything is clear. Your hand peels free from the door and the relief is overwhelming.

Then you look at your left hand and the space where your thumb used to be. It looks like the end of a cigarette after you light it. The burnt-off thumb scab stares back at you and you can't remember what you ate last night, but you see the yellow-neon bile and feel the burn as it leaves your throat. You feel as drunk as you've ever been before and then, without warning, the floor is closer than you'd like… you fight to stay awake, but your eyes have other ideas. They've seen enough.

* * *

It's your bed.

Your blankets.

The smell is the same one you always awaken to, only there's a mix of something else in the air - ammonia.

You're Mr. Piss-the-bed.

You move to get out of the pit of shame. Your pants stick to your thighs as you throw back the sheets and the smell hits your nostrils once again. When you swallow, the smell turns to taste and amplifies the pain in your throat.

As your right hand leaves your throat, you feel the dried yellow-neon bile on your T-shirt. Both hands rubbing your eyes to force them to open, something feels different.

You remember your thumb.

You look for your thumb.

You raise your left hand.

One, two, three, four fingers, but no thumb!

The scab stares back at you from where your thumb should be. It doesn't hurt and when you moved the tendons that were attached to it for so long, they still move… only without the flagpole, they once flew.

Mr. One-Thumb.

Did Ginny the Witch really grant you your wish?

Did she put you back in your bed?

Is she the reason you pissed yourself?

Is your bladder controlled by fear?

The fear of seeing an actual witch in the flesh. Long nose, warts, crooked back, and claw-like fingers here in your room. Leaving and taking the habit of dry sheets back with her - thirty-plus years gone with a click of a finger.

How will you ever click your left hand again?

The thought of your wish snaps into light, mixing with the sunlight of a new day. You remember standing outside the purple house. The not-so-toothless hole in the door. 'I want all women to fall madly in love with me whenever they lay eyes on me.' Was your lack of a thumb situation worth it? Will all women fall madly in love with you at first sight now? Is the dry spell over… and not in the piss-soaked bed-wetting way? The excitement takes over.

Shower, check.

Best clothes, check.

Heading out the door, check.

Mr. Irresistible?

Mr. Only-Time-Will-Tell.

* * *

There's nothing like desperately wanting to know if a magic spell has worked to get your blood going. You're four, five blocks away from your house, the pub is in sight and the hunt for a woman is on. Just one will do. One to walk in with you and show those bastards that it isn't just you and your hand. Your eyes move quicker than a child with a fifty to burn and a shit-ton of pick and mix in front of them. You're not even concerned with the flavours you just want a woman. Any shape, size or colour will do. You just need the magic to happen and one to walk in with you. One that will help wipe the smug grin from their faces.

Then the scream hits your ears and breaks through your thought process. It sounds otherworldly.

A dying fox?

An alien meeting a flamethrower?

A child witnessing a puppy getting run over?

It's a combination of all the above and it makes your blood run cold. You don't want to turn around, but another one starts as the crescendo of the first forces the hairs on the back of your neck to stand to attention. Now a chorus of screams reach your ears and the feeling in your stomach is telling you to move your legs, but you don't. Instead, you turn around and face the music.

Two women are running towards you at full speed. Both are better looking than anyone you've ever had the pleasure of before. Sheer joy fills their faces. They are screaming with anticipation as they get closer to their target.

The first doesn't care about the traffic or the man welding a chainsaw into his hedges. She only wants one thing. You. Even when she rushes into the road and the oncoming taxi clips her back leg, she doesn't stop running towards you; she doesn't even break her stride. She wants you and nothing else matters.

The second woman, considerably further behind the first, screams louder in desperation.

'He's MINE! Stay back, BITCH!'

She doesn't break her stride either, as she is too far behind already, but the rattle in her words scares you. She is a woman on a mission, and she is beautiful, too. Her long golden hair blowing in the wind looks like the sail to the ship of wonders that awaits you. You wonder how she tastes.

You look down at the place where your left thumb used to be. This is everything you ever imagined and more. These two fine women on your arm will be more than adequate chaperones as you walk into the pub and watch the three tormentors' jaws shatter on the floor. You're Mr. Confident, soon-to-be Mr. Legend.

The first woman is within touching distance now, but she isn't slowing down. She hits you with such force that she lifts you off your feet and you land on your back. She's sucking your neck like a leech and trying to force you free from your pants.

'I want you, baby! I need you inside of me!'

Her frantic panting in your ear couple with her warm wet tongue over your lips and her intense sucking of your neck feels incredible and you fight the urge to push her away. This stranger is making something happen downstairs. It's getting harder… literally… to fight the urge to resist, but as her forceful hand reaches down the front of your pants for your member, a firm hand in her hair tugs her backwards and one of her nails scratches the purple surface of your helmet.

You're the perfect mix of Mr. Horny, Mr. Wounded, and Mr. Bitterly-disappointed.

'I said he's mine, BITCH!'

The second woman has a fist full of your fondler's hair and is dragging her away from you. You struggle to your feet, pulling your pants up as you rise. The wet patches on your neck are already bruising. You can feel them rising under your skin. Love bites! You can't hide the glimmer of a smile.

'Ladies. Ladies. We can sort this, please.'

You play it smooth because you're trying to be Mr. Diplomatic-solution.

'Tell her your stuff is mine!' the fondler screams.

'Tell HER your seed is mine!' screams the other as she tries to remove a chunk of hair from your fondler's head.

The two women stare at you with an intensity like you've never experienced before. You feel naked. Two minutes ago, you were on the way to the pub to let those imbeciles watch as you walked in like the cat that found the recipe for cream. Now you're wondering how to stop two women from tearing one another apart! They are pulling each other's hair and clothes. Tearing at each other, scratching, punching, and biting. Limb and nails and teeth.

You look around for some moral support. The guy with the chainsaw has turned it off. Two men in a van have stopped the traffic as they settle in to watch the brutal catfight unfold. People have poured out of their houses to watch the bloodbath. That's when reality hits you. There are more women now. A fuck load more and they're all moving towards you. The fight caught their attention, but now they've seen the prize. The whole reason for the madness and now they are racing towards you with the same goal. They all want a piece of the prize.

A spray of warm liquid hits you in the face, some of which goes in your eye. You look at the chaos unfolding before you. Your fondler's ear is now in the runner's mouth and the blood is gushing from the open wound.

That's when you hear the three-headed torment machine.

'Hey! Look what we have here, boys! Fucking Ginny the Witch shagging scab head has only gone and paid two birds to scrap.'

'You sick pervert, this is how you get your kicks, is it?'

'What they prefer to pull each other's hair out than shag you, that it? Fuck! Is that a fucking ear?!'

You don't know which of the three is responsible for each comment because, in that moment, somebody jumps on your back, propelling you forward and into the fight. The two women turn their attention to you. The woman on your back has her arms and legs wrapped around your neck and waist and, as you fall to the ground, she cushions your landing. Your fondler lands on your front and is back to sucking on your neck, only this time the hot blood from her ear sprays over your face. The runner has stripped off her bottom half and her semi-naked body is tugging at your pants off; she is determined to be the victor in the race for your seed. The woman you landed on is whispering sweet nothings into your other ear as the blood continues to spurt onto your face.

'Don't worry, my love. I'll protect you.'

A fourth and fifth woman come into view, and you see that they too are stripping away their bottom halves. The fourth woman is larger than your first fondler and she, too, grabs a fist full of her hair. She uses it to force her away from your head and then she settles on your chest. Her weight is considerable, and you instantly struggle to breathe. Her top half is an oversized jumper, but the hairs on her legs bristle against your face as she moves her dripping reproductive organ closer to your mouth.

'Taste me! Taste me! You'll never need another. Taste me!'

The smell is worse than a sewer on a hot day in June. It's worse than a baby's shit-filled, rotting, nappy left in a stifling car on a warm summer's evening. It's worse than your dad's sweaty feet after a full day of hiking, only he forgot to wear socks. It's worse than that fish you couldn't find at the back of your fridge that time, you know, the one that decomposed before you found it. And it's heading for your mouth. You try to scream, but the weight on your chest won't allow it.

You turn your head away and see the three tormentors frozen in time. The chaos has shattered their jaws on the floor. They can't comprehend what their eyes are showing them.

They're speechless.

You feel the slimy, warm texture as it moves onto your neck, crushing and consuming your Adam's apple as tentacle-like damp flaps crawl up and onto your chin.

The animalistic noise of the zombified women trying to consume you stops as moist thighs engulf your ears.

You close your eyes as you feel the greasy, hairy stench reach your bottom lip.

The sunlight fades.

Then the weight becomes more bearable, and the smell fades. As you open your eyes, your body moves. You're being dragged by one of your tormentors, whilst the other two fight off the herd of women amassing around you. Fists are flying and blood is spilling everywhere, but they keep moving towards safety. It all feels like a horror movie as they eventually drag you into the pub and force the doors shut.

'Fuck! Fuck! What the fuck was all that about?'

'Jesus! They were trying to fucking consume you!'

The banging on the pub door forces you all back another few paces.

'That was mental! They're obsessed with you.'

Then a fourth voice stops them all from speaking.

The cackle is clear, and it stops your blood cold.

'That… Was a wish fulfilled. HAHAHAHAHAHAHAHAHA! Don't like it? Oh, poor ladies' man, want his old life back? Well… I do still need another thumb… HAHAHAHAHAHAHA… and the full moon is approaching. Just say the word, my dear, and they all disappear. Like you never even existed.'

Ginny the Witch moves out from behind the bar. She looks like an ambassador for every story you've ever heard about witches. Boils on her face. Long, crooked nose. Small arched frame. Black cloak. Grey, wiry hair. Long sharp fingers. She floats towards you.

You flinch and so do your saviours.

They're as quiet as three little church mice now.

A huge thunderous weight crashes against the pub doors, causing you all to flinch again.

'Well dear, they're thirsty, aren't they? Just stick out your other thumb and say… please, and I'll make it all better.'

Another thunderous weight smashes against the doors, splinters of wood escaped the door this time. Then another thud and you see a lone eye staring at you from the other side of the door. That eye is quickly pushed away, only to be replaced by another. Then another. Then another.

You stick out your right thumb.

You're Mr. Terrified.

Ginny the Witch smiles. That smile reveals sharp teeth. Teeth which cover all corners of her mouth like a great white. A burst of pain surges down your right arm as she severs your thumb from your hand. Then an intense flash of white light flickers and Ginny is gone.

You sit with the three church mice, who all stare in amazement at your thumbless hands. One of your saviours goes over to the bar. He pulls a pint and brings it over to you. He places the rim of the glass to your lips.

'Here you go, mate. You need this more than anyone.'

You sip the liquid, and it is the sweetest you've ever tasted.

You let the glow of the beer embrace you.

A tear runs down your face.

You've never been referred to as 'mate' before.

You smile.

You're thumbless.

You're womanless.

But you're Mr. Mate, and that's enough for you.

ABOUT THE AUTHOR

Chris Hooley lives in a house with his two children and fanciful partner Paige.

He can be found on the internet by typing in The Writing Community Chat Show into the search engine. There you'll see him talking to much better writers about the craft of writing.

He is the author of Death, Just Grin and Bear It (novel), The Covid Criminals (short stories collection) and in this particular collection Ginny the Witch Grants a Wish. His ultimate goal, in writing, is to have someone physically react to the words on the page… vomiting… fainting… just anything other than falling to sleep will do.

Meet Cute

Ross Young

*T*hese things happen when you're not expecting them. Don't look for love, son. As long as you're out there in the world, it'll look for you. Ah, I know what you're thinking, 'but dad, not everyone is as lucky as you and mam,' well, you're right there, son. Though, I'm pretty sure I got a lot luckier than your mam.

Well, I suppose I best tell you how it happened then.

I was new in town. Fresh-faced, bright-eyed, and bushy-tailed, or so they say. Anyway, the big city lights had called me and I was itching to find a job and make my way in the world. It was right in this here city. Stepping off the train into that glorious drizzle, the wind flapping my scarf into my face. Before I even knew what had happened, I was being corralled through the gates and harangued by some fella trying to sell me a newspaper.

You might not think it now, but it was pretty scary for someone as new to things as I was. Oh, you lot today, think you know it all, don't you? Well, my lad, I'll tell you this much for free. The phones back then didn't have all your wireless GPS and internet gobbledegook. I had to find my way around without them. Oh, aye, I see you thinking now, 'doesn't sound so bad.' No, well, you try putting your gadgets aside and see how far you get. When was the last time you used an old paper map? No? You've probably never even held one.

Back then though, well, I was starting from the bottom all ready to work my way up. I had nowt but the skin I was standing in, well, and the clothes. A few coins to rub together, and a whopping hundred pounds in the bank account to keep me going for the first few weeks. That's right, weeks, lad. Things were tight, and there was none of that frivolous spending. Nowadays, you wouldn't be able to subscribe to your Whosflix and your Rainforest Prime, or any of that stuff. Catch someone asking for avocado on toast, or four-shot double whipped cream macchiato with pumpkin spice and hazelnut, and you'd think they were from a different planet. You wouldn't catch me being daft like that. Internet? Pah, the only way you could get internet access was on an old-school modem that screamed at you like a banshee negotiating with the devil himself before it let you wait half an hour to check your email. So no. Looking for work online was out of the question.

What did I do? Well, I'll tell you. I marched right into the first pub I saw. Straight across from the station, it was. They had a little piece of paper in the window that said 'help wanted' and so I thought, well, I can be 'help', can't I? Give the people a bit of chat, hand them a drink, and Bob's your uncle... no, not that Bob, he's just weird, it's a saying, lad. Get your head out of your video games for a minute and you'd know that. Try a book or something... I'm not getting into this. I'm telling you something important, listen.

Your mother, now she was a mighty fine woman. Not the sort to be caught in a pub like that in the middle of the day. Though she and her mates weren't afraid of visiting places off the beaten track. She was a student up at the university. The posh one where the boffins and that go. They all went to their student-type places. No, son, not the sort of place the likes of me wanted to frequent.

I didn't know it at the time, but we were destined to meet.

That job in the pub? Well, they laughed me out of the place. I look back now and it was my fault. You've got to be confident and comfortable in your skin, and I just wasn't. The woman behind the bar said to me, 'you seem like a nice sort, but it's not up to me, it's up to them,' then she waved at the customers. The customers! Putting a lad like me on display like some kind of meat. Well, they made their feelings clear. You see, I wasn't ready yet.

Don't you tell me to get the point, you cheeky little… This is important. You've got to understand that we were from different worlds, your mother and me.

So, I'd landed in the city and been resoundingly rejected from my first attempt to get a job, and it was getting late. I was beginning to get a little worried. I was also getting more than a little peckish.

My old man, pftt… I look like a right soft lad compared to him. He said to me, 'son, you're best off not eating the first night you get there. Save every penny you've got, just in case.'

Hah, you're right, I said just the same thing to him, 'but dad, in case of what?' You're a chip off the old block sometimes, lad. Where was I? Ah, right, your mother.

Well, as it was getting dark I walked a bit further into town and found myself a Golden Arches, Maccy D's. Aye, they had it back then. How old do you think I am? Cheeky little sod.

Not to eat. I just explained what me Da said, didn't I? No, I went because there's always a job going there, and I'm not too proud to drop that stuff they call food into paper bags for a living. It's busy though. It's that time of day when people have knocked off from work. Outside it's pissing down, and who wants to sit on the bus on the way home freezing to death listening to knobheads scream at each other while you're sandwiched into a seat next to a bloke who smells like he's pissed himself? Nobody, exactly. So people figure, I'll get a bit of tea first, a quick bit of scran, it saves on cooking, and it's cheap as chips, well… it is chips.

They used to have this Monopoly game where you collected the little stickers and filled them in to get free stuff. Do they still do that? No. It was good, that was. Alright, calm down, I'm getting to it. What's your rush? Oh, right, well you can join your clan for whatever it is in a bit. Oh, and none of that incognito browsing, you know what I mean with that fake tentacle stuff, it's weird, lad.

I was there, not knowing what to do with myself, so I got in the queue. Kept my head down, as there was some rowdiness and I'm just this bag of bones about to beg for a job, well, fill in an application form and hope they were desperate.

It was taking ages. Do you ever get that feeling that something's about to happen? You know the one, feel it right there, in your guts. The tension in the room. Aye, like just before your team concedes a goal. You know it's going to happen, but there's nothing you can do about it. Well, it were building proper like.

I'm standing there, hands in my pockets, giving it the shifty eye to make sure I wasn't about to get in someone's way or become the target for someone needing to show off.

A gust of wind comes through the door. It sends a bunch of napkins flying, and some numpty drops a big cup of coke or something. It splashed all over the floor. All the people in there give out one of those roars, you know, the sarcastic 'wahay!' As if everyone's already had a few drinks.

They're all moving around, arms up in the air. Someone's shouting at someone else for getting their new trainers wet. Yeah, some things never change, son. Me though? Well, I'm watching the door when she walks in. Your mother. She was spectacular. She still is, as far as I'm concerned. Oh, I know she's your mother. Don't get yourself worked up. We were young once though, son.

She's tottering in high heels like she's on a brand-new pair of legs and doesn't know how to use them. Standing in between her friends and surveying the people inside like she's not got a care in the world, next to nothing on, pfft, well neither of us has ever really felt the cold, you don't either.

All my efforts of keeping myself quiet, not being noticed. Well, they went right out the window. I couldn't take my eyes off her, and some clever tit, you know the type. I mean, you and your mates have probably been the type at some point. Well, this lad sitting with his mates, all suited up like a right toff, probably an estate agent or something… No, I don't think there's anything wrong with being an estate agent, son, I'm just trying to paint you a picture. You know what I mean. It's not offensive, is it? Is that not PC, or woke, to call someone an estate agent? I can't bloody keep up anymore. Oh, so it's fine. Well then, he looked like he might have been an estate agent. I bet he drove a BMW or an Audi, too. Oh, let it go, son, you want an Audi, go get an Audi. Let me tell the story.

So this bloke, who was wearing a very nice suit and might have been anything from a candlestick maker to a baker for all I knew. Are you happy now? Good. He stands up, points at me, and shouts, "check out gormless here. I think he might like you, love."

Well, it made me feel like a right knobber. I think if it hadn't been so busy, and I hadn't been so desperate for a job, I might have torn him apart. Oh, I remember what it was like to be young and hotheaded. We've all been there once upon a time. I'll give that younger version of me some credit though. I didn't do it. Instead, I just grinned, looked at the Est… ahem, the nicely dressed man, and said, 'congratulations on having a life so small you spend your evenings observing other people doing the things you wish you could.' It wasn't the best line, but it made your mother and her friends laugh. Of course, that only made the man in the suit and his mates even more annoyed.

See, what I did then, unwittingly, was escalate the situation. You don't want to do that if you can help it, son. You want to try to de-escalate things. Now people were looking at me. This bedraggled, skinny whelp standing in the queue, looking for a job, was now the centre of attention. I was in trouble because this suit fella and his mates were getting all puffed up. You know, all desperate to prove they were alpha males. People are like that, aren't they?

Your mother, though, she was as sharp as a tack, quick as a flash she says, "thanks for saving us a place in the queue, love. How was your day?" She comes over and grabs my hand.

Don't look so shocked, she was a right spitfire back then. Still is now. Remember when you got in trouble with that coach? She soon sorted him, didn't she? Yeah, well. Suit gets a look on his face like he's swallowed a handful of wasps, but he sits down and tries to ignore us. Takes a bit of a hard time from his friends, but he'll survive to cause trouble… for a bit longer.

Now I'm stuck in the queue holding the hand of the most beautiful stranger I've ever seen. I tell her thanks, but I'm really embarrassed. She knew I was staring, then she squeezes my hand a little tighter. "I thought it was for the best," she says. "Wouldn't want you making a mess of the place."

Her friends are there, two girls. Can't even remember their names now, your mother will, but it's not important. We stood in that queue and she wouldn't let go of my hand until we got to the front. Then she asks me what I'm having and I tell her I'm not hungry, I'm actually applying for a job. I don't know what possessed me to say it, but I tell her I'm not really keen on fast food and she laughs.

I suppose I looked like a right dafty. Standing in the queue to apply for a job and I don't even like the place. Then she gives me a wink. Not a subtle one either. "I'm the same."

That floored me. Properly knocked me for six, son. She didn't mean, 'I'm the same' about the food. She meant 'I'm the same,' about everything. Well, there was nothing for it then.

"I'm going to make a mess of things," I said. Your mother laughed. Oh, how she laughed. It silenced the whole place.

At that exact moment, well, I suppose technically just after that exact moment because she'd already said it… All hell broke loose.

The lights flickered, the doors locked, and everyone inside panicked. As well they should.

I don't know what came over me, son. A sudden urge and I knew I wasn't comfortable in my skin anymore, and your mother didn't look comfortable in hers, and then both of us just decided to Hell with it.

I tore off my flesh right in the middle of the restaurant. Bursting through the skin. I bunched up my tentacles and smashed my way through the poor sap I was inhabiting like he was made of paper. Ribs cracking, muscles bursting, the spine tore out the back and ripped clean through those cheap clothes. Flesh and bone were torn asunder. It splattered across the faces of customers who were frozen in shock as I reached out in every direction. I slithered into their waiting gaping mouths, forcing my way up through their nasal cavities, and tore out their grey matter using the tips of my tentacles. Swirling it up and yanking it out before offering it to your mother.

Her body, which was a nice one as well, tore from the top of her head right down her middle and it just fell to either side. A pair of dull, fleshy slaps as it hit the floor, and she writhed out of it in her glorious natural form. The two friends on either side of her were lifted off the floor and your mother shoved their heads clean through the ceiling tiles. Their feet kicked and twitched for ages afterward like marionettes with their strings caught in the breeze.

Our tentacles met over the crawling screaming humans while they scrambled towards the doors. Of course, there was no escape. We'd pulled the old telepathic rune lock on them. Their screams, a right cacophony, were the siren that ushered in our love. While they wailed sobbing, over the speakers the music played. The song was 'It must be love' by Madness, I still get misty-eyed, well eye, thinking about it now. The flickering lights cast a pallid glow over her dripping palps as our antennae interlocked. Her suckers squelched in time to the music while she popped open heads like bursting watermelons. It's still music to my ears now, son.

In seconds, the windows to the shop were so covered in blood it looked like it had been painted red from the inside. People probably thought the place had gone out of business. Oh, that was a bloody day when we threw off our hosts and consummated our love, forming the glorious eye of Karak-Som-Tirek-Qwa.

As we reached the end, we realised what a mess we had made. Oh, how we laughed as time stood still and we gorged on the bodies of the hapless humans. All things must come to an end, though. We reached out, tentacles entwined, staring into one another's eye while we secreted out our digestive juices until every inch of the restaurant was covered in a layer of our combined mucous. Then, together as one, we sucked in our first dinner together through our thousand mouths to fill the darkness of the void within.

I don't think we've ever had a meal that has come close. Well, to be fair, there was that curry house when we went on holiday to Brighton, but I still think they skimped on the naan bread.

Oh, right, of course, that was the end of those hosts. Sorry, son, got a bit carried away then. You shouldn't be embarrassed about stuff like that though, it's perfectly natural.

Luckily for us, the estate agent had somehow avoided the worst of our fevered attacks. He was still conscious, quivering with his feet up on a chair while he wept and made these strange little bleating noises. It did give me a chuckle before I forced myself through his orifices, spitting out the contents of his skin so I could take over his body. Well, son, I did say it was a nice suit.

Your mother, sharp as ever, made her way into the body of the manager. She gave me my first job; I mean after we had cleared the place thoroughly and made sure that any missed remains were ground up into burgers and the such-like.

Oh, aye? Well, there's a pentagram on the floor of that Maccy's now which we used to summon Valragdien the devourer and he swept up the mess. Our parents were over the moon. They didn't even know there were two of us in the same region, never mind a potential mating couple. Seven years later, on the night of a blood moon, we took you, our firstborn, to the summoning ceremony. While some kind humans read from the book of annihilation, we opened a rip in the veil and forced you into the body of their lovely, innocent sacrifice. By all accounts, he was a very nice young lad as well, filled with promise. Not literally. He was filled with the usual stuff, liver, kidneys, and whatnot. Then you fed on the robed followers just like a growing lad should.

I remember it like it was yesterday. Of course, you moved on to unindoctrinated food soon enough, only so long you can keep little 'uns feasting on the converted.

See what I was saying, son? Don't look for love, son, it'll find you. Somewhere on this side of the void or the other, there'll be someone wearing a meat suit waiting to bump into another meat suit. We void travelling creatures of horror and damnation have a way of being drawn to one another. I think it's got something to do with where these cults crop up, to be honest, must be a regional thing.

The point of the story?

Oh, right? Well, you remember that monopoly game I said they had? Well, your mother had collected a whole one and had given it to friends to use. Yeah, looks like they never passed go. Anyway, that's why we took the name Fenchurch, after Fenchurch Street station. That's why you're Azmorgardiel Vindictivus Fenchurch. Isn't that what you asked?

No?

Why did you ask?

What do you mean you never bloody asked? Get on with you, cheeky little sod. Oh, and if you're going out, your mother needs eggs, and get me a Mars Bar. Footy's on the telly later, big match, don't be late.

ABOUT THE AUTHOR

Ross Young lives in France with his wife, daughter, and a pair of hounds of disrepute. He was born in Newcastle Upon Tyne in a hospital that has since been knocked down.

He has authored three books; Dead Heads, Get Ted Dead, and Dead Festive, with book four of Gloomwood novels Dead Culture coming soon.

His writing has been described as; ridiculous, funny, weird, and macabre. Despite his appearance and demeanour, he does not write from experience. He also draws silly comics featuring Beelzebub and the Grim Reaper.

You can find him @ryoungsulk on twitter.

Or visit his website rossyoung.ink

Acknowledgements

 This anthology could not have happened without the hard work and dedication of the team behind it. Each of the authors involved has given an incredible amount of their own time and effort into ensuring the stories within it are fantastic, but also that the anthology as a whole is something we can all be proud of. So in no particular order, a huge thank you to; Halo Scot, A.C. Merkel, Kayla Hicks, Peter James Martin, Melissa Rodgers, SJ Covey, Rose J Fairchild, Chris Hooley, NT Anderson, Evelyn Chartres, Jon Ford, Samantha Kroese.

Each of them has now had a fraction of their essence removed and bottled in a cursed flask. A tiny portion of them will forever languish on the topmost shelf of Malarkey's shelves of solitude, where it will remain forever more. Their muted screams harmonising to from Malarkey's own unique brand of ASMR sleep sounds.

Malarkey's ImaginOmnibus

Malarkey's ImaginOmnibus will be back soon...

www.ingramcontent.com/pod-product-compliance
Lightning Source LLC
Chambersburg PA
CBHW021954170726
47994CB00021B/355